This month we are delighted to present a special selection of six classic stories in four books (two 2-in-1s and two singles) from your favourite Mills & Boon® Medical™ Romance authors!

This exclusive bestselling author
collection includes:

THE CELEBRITY DOCTOR'S PROPOSAL
by Sarah Morgan
with
A MOTHER BY NATURE
by Caroline Anderson

THE SURGEON'S GIFT
by Carol Marinelli
with
BUSHFIRE BRIDE
by Marion Lennox

EARTHQUAKE BABY by Amy Andrews

TWICE AS GOOD by Alison Roberts

D1427192

TWICE AS GOOD

BY
ALISON ROBERTS

First published in Great Britain 2000. This edition 2013.
by Mills & Boon, an imprint of Harlequin (UK) Limited,
Eton House, 18-24 Paradise Road, Richmond, Surrey TW9 1SR

© Alison Roberts 2000

ISBN: 978 0 263 90660 8
ebook ISBN: 978 1 472 01220 3

03-0613

Harlequin (UK) policy is to use papers that are natural, renewable and recyclable products and made from wood grown in sustainable forests. The logging and manufacturing processes conform to the legal environmental regulations of the country of origin.

Printed and bound in Spain
by Blackprint CPI, Barcelona

Alison Roberts lives in Christchurch, New Zealand, and has written over sixty Mills & Boon® Medical™ Romances. As a qualified paramedic she has personal experience of the drama and emotion to be found in the world of medical professionals, and loves to weave stories with this rich background—especially when they can have a happy ending. When Alison is not writing you'll find her indulging her passion for dancing or spending time with her friends (including Molly the dog) and her daughter Becky, who has grown up to become a brilliant artist. She also loves to travel, hates housework, and considers it a triumph when the flowers outnumber the weeds in her garden.

Recent titles by Alison Roberts:

CHAPTER ONE

IT HAD to be the Monday morning from hell.

The aggressive burst of steam that escaped as the autoclave hatch opened clutched viciously at Janet Muir's fingers. She dropped the stainless steel tongs she was holding and swore softly but vehemently.

'You should open the door a bit more slowly.'

Janet's gaze flew to the speaker. 'Thank you, Dr Spencer.' Her tone was unappreciative. She snatched the tongs from the floor. 'If I had ten seconds to spare I would have done exactly that.'

'Sorry, Jan.' Oliver Spencer's smile was contrite. 'Is your hand OK?'

'Only third-degree burns. I'll live.' Janet pulled the tray clear of the autoclave and deposited it onto the waiting towel.

'Has that lab result on Jessica Andrews come through yet? She still hasn't shown much improvement and I think we'll need to change antibiotics.'

'Try the fax machine,' Janet suggested. 'I haven't had time to look yet. I had no idea how chaotic things would be with both Josh and Toni away on their honeymoon. Has Dr Singh arrived yet?'

'No.' Oliver Spencer looked worried. 'I'm just going to try ringing her again. Did she usually turn up on time when she was doing that week's locum for me?'

'Always. In fact, Toni told me she asked for a key so she could turn up early.'

Oliver glanced at his watch. 'I wouldn't call 10 a.m. early. I'll give her a call while I'm in the office.' Oliver turned away, then paused. 'On second thoughts, I'll do it in my room. Who *is* making that racket?'

'Sophie's next patient.' Janet sighed. The wailing of a fractious baby was a sound that would get on anyone's nerves in ten seconds flat. The staff of St David's Medical Centre had been subjected to ten minutes' worth so far. 'Maybe Dr Singh will arrive any minute and rescue us.'

There was no sign of any assistance when Janet hurried back into the main office a few minutes later. The young receptionist, Sandy Smith, was looking harassed.

'I can't find the file for Joshua Young anywhere and he's Sophie's next patient.'

'Try Josh's office,' Janet advised. 'There are often a few files lurking in a corner. Has Oliver had any luck tracking down our locum yet?'

'No.' Sandy bit her lip and looked even more harassed. 'I'm supposed to ring the agency. I got distracted, hunting for that baby's file. He won't stop crying and the phone never stops ringing. See?' Sandy pointed to the offending device as the telephone rang to illustrate her point.

'I'll get it.' Janet grinned. 'You go and see if you can find the file. Don't worry too much if you can't. I'm sure Sophie will cope.'

Janet dealt quickly with the phone call. She was

about to summon her next patient when Oliver beckoned from the office doorway.

'I've got May Little in my room. Could you do a repeat ECG on her, please?'

'You're kidding!' Janet's dismay was evident. 'I've got an eighteen-month check and immunisation waiting, and Mrs Endicott is here early for her iron shot and blood test. Miss Little's ECG last Friday took me half an hour!'

The patient's name was ironically inappropriate. May Little was morbidly obese and the undergarments she used to try and give her bulk some semblance of shape made Janet think of attempts on Fort Knox. She was also a rather odd lady and Janet sighed at the prospect of another encounter so soon.

'Is she undressed?' she asked Oliver pointedly.

Oliver was backing out of the office rapidly. 'Not quite. I'll send her down to you.'

'Can't *you* do it?' Janet pleaded, but Oliver was now conveniently out of hearing range. Janet stepped out of the office and stood beneath the archway that separated the waiting room from the hallway. 'Sorry, Mrs Endicott. I'll be a few minutes yet.'

'I've got an appointment with my hairdresser at eleven. I can't wait *all* day, dear.'

Janet smiled apologetically. Sandy appeared in the hallway, waving a manila case file triumphantly, and Janet's smile brightened. 'Good for you,' she congratulated her.

The front door opened as the telephone rang yet again. Janet hesitated but went back into the office to help Sandy cope for a minute. The new arrival was a woman who was balancing a child on one hip.

'I'm Ruth Prendergast,' she told Janet. 'I haven't got an appointment and we don't even live in Christchurch. We're just down here visiting my mother but Katy has been to see Dr Cooper once before and she's really not very well this morning.'

'What's the problem?' Janet smiled at the girl who did look rather pale.

'I think she's running a temperature and she won't eat or drink anything. She's unusually quiet as well. I know it's probably nothing but Katy has had a heart murmur since birth and I do tend to worry about her.'

'Did Dr Cooper know of her medical history?'

'Oh, yes. He was marvellous. He even rang her doctor in Auckland to check up on things.'

'How long ago would it have been since you saw Dr Cooper?'

'I think it was about this time last year.'

Sandy had finished her call. Janet pointed at a row of files separated from the main system. 'See if you can find a file for Katy Prendergast amongst the casuals there.' Janet turned back to Katy's mother. 'We'll get someone to look at Katy as soon as we can, but I'm afraid you might have a bit of a wait. As you can see, we're rather busy. Dr Cooper is away on his honeymoon and our locum hasn't shown up yet.' Janet heard Sandy groan behind her.

'Oh, no! I *still* haven't rung the agency.'

Ruth Prendergast was smiling. 'I don't mind waiting. I feel a lot better just being somewhere close to medical assistance.'

Janet nodded and smiled. 'Make yourselves comfortable. There are plenty of books and toys.' She could see Miss Little standing outside the office door. She was clutching a solid-looking handbag. A tight hat was jammed on her head and her thick woollen coat was firmly buttoned. Not quite undressed, indeed!

Janet ushered her patient into the treatment room and closed the door behind them. 'We'll need to get you undressed, Miss Little, so I can take the ECG.' Janet briskly pulled the curtain to screen the bed from the door.

'Did you know that you have a *cat* in your waiting room?'

'Yes. That's Outboard. St David's sort of acquired him quite recently. Did you not see him when you came in on Friday? He loves talking to people in the waiting room.'

'I don't like cats.' Miss Little had made no move to start undressing. 'They carry germs.'

'We don't let him come in here,' Janet said reassuringly. 'This is the only place we keep sterile equipment.' She reached out an encouraging hand to relieve her patient of the handbag. 'Have you been getting some more chest pain?'

Miss Little backed away, a protective arm now enclosing the handbag. 'Germs travel. They can go a very long way.'

'Not this far.' Janet decided to take a firm approach. 'Just take off everything down to your petticoat for me, Miss Little. Like you did on Friday.' Janet collected syringes, a vacutainer and tourniquet as she spoke. She opened a small cupboard to extract an ampoule of injectable iron solution. 'I'll be back in a minute or two, when you're all ready.' Janet moved briskly. She could do Mrs Endicott's test and treatment in the side room. At least that would be one empty seat in the waiting area.

Mrs Endicott was delighted at the unexpectedly prompt attention.

'It's not that I like to make a nuisance of myself,' she explained to Janet. 'I don't even want to go to the hairdresser today. It's far too nice a day to sit around for hours having a perm.'

'It *is* a lovely day,' Janet agreed. She tied the tourniquet around Mrs Endicott's upper arm. 'Just squeeze your hand for me a few times.'

'A perfect drying day,' Mrs Endicott continued contentedly. 'Monday's always been my washing day.'

'Every day's my washing day.' Janet deftly inserted the needle and clicked the vacutube into the plastic holder. 'But not today, unfortunately. I turned the washing machine on this morning and the next thing I knew I had a flood on the laundry floor.'

'Oh, dear! You've got two little boys, too, haven't you?'

'Yes. Twins. Adam and Rory.' Janet removed the full test tube and then pressed a cotton ball to Mrs Endicott's elbow as she withdrew the needle. 'They're six. Nearly seven.'

'You must have a lot of washing to do, then.'

'Heaps.' Janet agreed ruefully. She thought of the pile of muddy jeans, track pants and sweatshirts she had walked out on this morning, and sighed deeply. 'In fact, it's quite unbelievable how many items of clothing two small boys can go through over a weekend. If I don't get the machine fixed tonight, they may well have to go to school tomorrow in their pyjamas.' Janet picked up a syringe. 'Let's get this injection over with and that'll be you. I'll ring you when we get the results of this sample and let you know when we need to check your levels again. Hopefully, we're getting your anaemia under control now.'

Miss Little eyed the blood sample Janet carried back into the treatment room for labelling.

'I hope you're not intending to take any blood from me.'

'Dr Spencer hasn't ordered any blood tests, Miss Little. I think he wants to see the trace of your heart first.' Janet looked disbelievingly at May Little's foundation garment. Was it an antique or did they still manufacture genuine corsets? 'Can we undo this lacing bit on the front?' Janet struggled to keep her face straight. 'I need to stick an electrode on just about here.' She touched what felt like some steel reinforcement.

'You just never know, do you?'

'What about, Miss Little?'

'What they *do* with the blood. What they *really* test it for.'

'Oh, I don't think they do anything they're not asked to.' Janet clipped the electrodes into place on the sticky patches. 'They haven't got the time and it's all too expensive these days.'

May Little looked unconvinced. 'They already

know too much,' she informed Janet knowingly. 'They're not going to get any of *my* blood.'

'Mmm.' Janet ripped off the rhythm strip. If Miss Little needed a blood test Janet was going to make sure it was Oliver who did the deed. 'Stay here for a moment, Miss Little. I'll just get Dr Spencer to have a look at this.'

Oliver was pacing around his consulting room. 'Would you believe it?' he demanded of Janet incredulously. 'The locum agency just rang to ask if we'd had the message from Dr Singh. Apparently her mother took ill and she flew back to India yesterday. They wait until 11 a.m. and then ring to ask if we want someone else.'

'What did you say?'

'I said of course we want someone else. We wanted someone else at 9 a.m. *Before* the waiting room started overflowing.'

Janet winced at the choice of vocabulary. She would have to find time to ring a washing-machine repair firm or she would be in trouble tomorrow morning. Oliver was still speaking distractedly.

'Poor Sophie's not feeling at all well herself. She threw up three times before we even got to work.'

'She's got the written exam for her GP registration tomorrow, hasn't she? Is it nerves, do you think?'

'No.' Oliver couldn't suppress a grin as he reached for the ECG trace Janet was holding outstretched. 'We're pregnant.'

Janet gasped in surprise. 'I didn't even think of *that*!'

'Neither did we.' Oliver was still grinning. 'Toni

did. She thought that was why Sophie was so tired and hungry all the time, but she didn't miss a period. Twice. They were a lot lighter, she said, but they were still on time. You could have bowled us both over when we got the results of the blood test. I talked a mate into doing a scan over the weekend and it turns out she's about ten weeks along.'

Janet was nodding vigorously. 'The same thing happened to me. Exactly. Only I didn't find out until I was twelve weeks pregnant. Gave the father enough time to swan off and get someone else pregnant.'

'You're joking!' Oliver's face was a picture of disgust. 'I never knew. What a bastard!'

'You said it.' Janet tried to lighten the atmosphere with a grin. 'No wonder I was put off men for life, was it? No chance now, even if the twins *are* desperate for a father.'

'Did he know about the twins?'

'No.' Janet looked thoughtful. 'I was going to tell him but there didn't seem much point when I found out about the other woman.' Janet laughed without a trace of amusement. 'She was my best friend, would you believe?'

Oliver didn't look amused either. 'We're not all like that, Jan. You'll find the right person one of these days.'

'That's the problem, Oliver,' Janet said sadly. She kept her gaze on the ECG strip which Oliver appeared to have forgotten he was holding. 'I thought I *had* found the right person. I was so sure of it. Now I'll never be able to trust my own judgment again.' She managed another smile. 'Anyway, I'm so pleased about you and Sophie. That's great news.'

'Thanks. We're delighted. At least, *I'm* delighted and I'm sure Sophie will be, too, when she stops throwing up all the time.' Oliver finally spread the trace out beside the one already on his desk. 'That's good.' He nodded seconds later. 'No change at all. Tell her to come back in as soon as she's dressed.'

'You've probably got time for a coffee,' Janet told him dryly. 'Or you could have a quick look at a wee girl in the waiting room. She's a casual, in town visiting her grandmother, but she's been here before to see Josh. She's running a fever and is anorexic. She's also got a cardiac history of some kind.'

'OK. Put her in the side room and I'll be there in a minute. I hope we don't get too many casuals today.'

'What did the agency say in the end?'

'They'll send someone else. When or if they can find someone. There's a heavy demand for locums at present. Apparently we're in the middle of conference season.'

Luckily, Miss Little had decided to dress herself again without waiting for clearance. Janet despatched her towards Oliver's room. There was an unusual silence in the waiting area as she headed back to the front office. All conversation had stopped. Sandy was staring over the counter, looking slightly pale. Janet's nose provided the first clue to the new development to the day. Young Katy Prendergast had vomited, dousing both the carpet and the contents of the toy

basket. Eighteen-month-old Toby Dawson was openly
fascinated. Katy's mother was appalled.

'Oh, I'm *so* sorry! Can I find something to clean
up with?'

'I'll do that,' Janet told her. 'Don't worry. These
things happen.' She nudged Sandy. 'Take Katy and
her mum down to the side room. Get one of the cardboard containers out of my dressings cupboard in case
Katy feels sick again.'

Joshua Young's mother emerged from Sophie
Bennett's room. Joshua was still howling and his
mother looked weary. Her expression changed and
her nose wrinkled with distaste as she moved towards
the counter. Sophie followed her patient out. Her eyes
widened in dismay as she neared the waiting room,
then she clapped her hand over her mouth and nose
and ran for the toilet, slamming the door hurriedly
shut behind her.

Janet donned gloves and quickly gathered a bucket
of hot water and disinfectant, tucking a supply of floor
cloths under her arm. Toby's mother was trying to
keep the active toddler away from the toy basket.

'Take him into the treatment room, Margaret,'
Janet suggested. 'I won't be long. Sorry to have kept
you waiting.'

'No problem.' Toby's mother smiled. 'You look
like you're having a bad morning.'

Janet nodded wearily. There were still three people
left in the waiting room after Margaret and Toby left.
One was waiting to see Sophie who had still not
emerged from the toilet. May Little was in Oliver's
room and Katy was next in line for his attention. The

elderly Mr Beaumont and his wife would have to wait a while longer for their appointment to see Dr Spencer.

Sandy Smith looked ready to cry. 'I wish Toni was here,' she told Janet mournfully. 'I don't think I'm ready to cope with this job on my own. I'm only a receptionist, not a practice manager.'

'You're not on your own,' Janet told her. 'I'm here. And this is as bad as it gets around here. Honestly! If you can cope with this, you can cope with anything.'

Sandy sniffed dubiously and Janet patted her arm. 'Open the windows in here for a while. As soon as I've finished with wee Toby I'll come back and look after the desk and you can have half an hour for lunch. Take a walk by the river and get some sunshine and fresh air.'

Sandy brightened. 'I could go down to the shops. Outboard's getting low on cat food and kitty litter.'

Janet eyed the still firmly closed door of the toilet. 'Get some water crackers as well. They're supposed to be good for morning sickness.'

Not that there was much of the morning left. Toby and his mother had been waiting for over an hour for their appointment.

'I'm so sorry,' Janet apologised again. 'It's been chaos this morning. I don't think we had any idea how disruptive it was going to be, having both Josh and Toni away at the same time. *And* our locum didn't show up.'

'I'm not bothered,' Margaret assured her. 'It's not

often I get the chance to sit and read magazines. Where did Josh and Toni go for their honeymoon?'

'They're cruising the Caribbean,' Janet said with mock bitterness. 'If they send a postcard of some tropical paradise with "wish you were here" scribbled on the back, it will definitely be the last straw.'

Both women laughed, and Toby beamed at the sound. Janet held out her hand.

'Come and stand by the giraffe, sweetheart. Let's see how tall you've got.'

She recorded the measurement on Toby's file. 'He's shot up,' she told Margaret. 'That's a huge increase since his fifteen-month check.'

'Goodness knows where he's getting the energy to grow from. I can't get him to eat a thing.'

'Tell me about it,' Janet said with a grin. 'The fight I had this morning, trying to get my boys to eat breakfast!'

'You mean they haven't grown out of it yet?'

'It gets worse when they start watching TV,' Janet warned. 'All the ads for the new high-sugar, high-fat, junk cereal they keep coming up with. It's a constant battle.'

'So what do you give the twins for breakfast?'

'Porridge,' Janet said defensively. 'It was good enough for me when I was growing up and I wasn't even allowed brown sugar and milk on it.' She lifted Toby onto the scales.

'Toby likes porridge.' Margaret sighed. 'It's the meat and vegetables I can't get into him.'

'You're obviously doing quite well enough.' Janet steadied the toddler before checking the reading.

'He's right up the charts for both weight and height.' She lifted Toby onto the bed and tickled a smile out of her small patient. 'Do you like porridge, then, Toby?'

Toby nodded happily.

'I wish my boys did. They say it's got too many toenails in it.'

Toby looked nonplussed. So did Margaret. 'Toenails?'

'They're just the oat husks,' Janet explained. 'I make the real stuff that you have to soak overnight. It's healthier, not to mention a lot cheaper.' She unbuttoned the fastening on the shoulder of Toby's bright blue jersey. 'We'll take this off, shall we, darling? Dr Sophie is going to come and listen to your chest in a minute and look in your ears and down your throat. Do you think she'll be able to see the porridge *you* had for breakfast?'

Toby nodded gleefully. He stuck his arms up helpfully as Janet pulled the sleeves of his jersey clear. She excused herself to fetch Sophie but was waylaid by Sandy, who spoke in a whisper.

'That funny little man that looks like a garden gnome just came in.'

'Mr Collins?'

Sandy nodded. 'He hasn't got an appointment but he says the doctors will want to see him urgently. What shall I say?'

Janet sighed. Mr Collins was a regular patient. Too regular. 'What are his symptoms today?'

'He says he's got a crushing central chest pain radiating to his jaw and left arm. He's sweating and nauseated and he's having palpy something or other.'

'Palpitations.' Janet chuckled. 'You'll have to borrow Mr Collins's textbook some time. He doesn't need it any more. I think he's learned off every symptom by heart.' Janet pondered the situation briefly. 'Tell him to have a seat. Maybe I can keep him happy by taking his blood pressure and doing an ECG. He hasn't picked a very good day to come looking for a bit of attention, has he?'

Sophie hadn't quite finished with her patient. She still looked wan as she came into the treatment room ten minutes later.

'I like powwidge,' Toby informed Sophie. 'Wiv toenails.'

Sophie gave Janet a despairing glance and rushed out of the room. Janet had to laugh. 'I don't believe this. Let me see if Oliver can come and see Toby. Sophie might be held up for a while. She's in a rather delicate state.'

It was another fifteen minutes before Margaret was able to take Toby home for his lunch. Sandy took the opportunity to escape for her break and Janet tidied up the treatment room, before moving back to the main office to man the telephones. It was only then that she remembered Mr Collins. He was sitting quietly in the corner of the waiting room. Too quietly.

'Oliver!' Janet shouted. 'Sophie! Come quickly!'

Janet Muir's strength was out of proportion to her slim build. She had no real difficulty transferring Mr Collins to the floor. She had tilted his head back to open his airway and was feeling his neck for the carotid pulse as both doctors rushed in.

'No pulse, no respirations,' she reported. Pinching the elderly man's nose, Janet covered his mouth with her own and inflated his lungs with two deep, full breaths.

Oliver positioned his hands on Mr Collins's chest to begin cardiac compressions. 'Grab the life pack,' he directed Sophie. 'And a bag mask unit.'

Sophie was back within seconds. She stuck the electrodes in place and Oliver stopped compressions while they looked at the screen.

'Ventricular fibrillation,' Oliver muttered. Sophie had the large sticky pads ready as Oliver cut through Mr Collins's clothing. He positioned the paddles. 'Everybody clear,' he instructed.

Janet lifted the mask away from skin contact. Sandy walked in just as Mr Collins' body jerked in response to the electrical shock.

'Oh, my God!' she said in horror.

'Grab the oxygen cylinder from my room, Sandy,' Janet called. 'And then call an ambulance. Mr Collins has had a cardiac arrest.'

Sandy dropped the tins of cat food and the large bag of kitty litter by the front door. She ran to collect the oxygen cylinder.

'Good girl,' Janet said calmly. 'Now call the ambulance.'

Sandy backed away, staring as Oliver raised the paddles again. 'Charging to 360 joules,' he stated. 'Sophie, get an IV line in as soon as you can and draw up one milligram of adrenaline. Janet, find some lignocaine and some more adrenaline.'

Janet opened the drug cupboard in the treatment room hurriedly to locate the requested drugs. She could hear the wail of the ambulance siren in the distance. She could also hear the loud knocking on the front door. Hoping that Sandy would have the initiative not to allow an early afternoon patient to stumble in on the emergency, Janet grabbed some extra IV supplies and headed back.

'I'm sorry,' she heard Sandy calling loudly, 'but we can't see any patients just yet. We're in the middle of an—'

Janet saw the door being pushed open firmly. 'I'm not a patient,' she heard the visitor assert. 'I'm the locum. My God, what's going on in here?'

'Cardiac arrest,' Oliver stated tersely. 'Come and take over the compressions, would you?'

The newcomer moved swiftly. Janet found herself staring at his back as he crouched over Mr Collins. His hands were positioned unerringly, his compressions smoothly confident. 'How much adrenaline has he had?'

'Three doses of one milligram so far.'

'What about a bolus dose of lignocaine?'

Janet handed the ampoule to Oliver and stepped back. Sophie was ventilating Mr Collins, using the bag mask unit, now attached to high-flow oxygen. Janet stood behind the newcomer, listening to his verbal exchanges with Oliver, thankful she wasn't needed any closer just now. She was aware of her skin prickling all over. Every word uttered by this man sent a new shiver down her spine.

'How long has CPR been in progress?'

Oliver glanced at the clock. 'Ten minutes.' He injected the dose of lignocaine.

'Was the collapse witnessed?'

'Not exactly.' Sophie was squeezing the bag on the mask automatically. 'Mr Collins was sitting in the waiting room for a while by himself. He was pulseless but not cyanosed when he was found.' Sophie glanced up at Janet who bit her lip.

She knew how it would sound. Patients dropping dead in a doctor's waiting room unnoticed wasn't exactly a great recommendation for a medical centre. It would seem even worse when it was known that Mr Collins had come in describing the classic symptoms of a heart attack. How could she explain that this patient had turned up repeatedly over the years with the classic symptoms of every ailment known to man. That he'd had baseline cardiological investigations only weeks ago which hadn't revealed any pathology. That their experienced practice manager, who would have instinctively picked up a genuine emergency, was at present on the other side of the world. The bare facts of the emergency would present a picture of a medical centre that wasn't up to scratch. Janet didn't want this locum to have that as his first impression of St David's.

'Let's give this another shot.' Oliver pushed a button on the life pack. 'Charging to 360 joules again. If this doesn't do anything, we'll intubate.'

The ambulance crew arrived as the interference on

the monitor screen settled. The spikes of an effective heart rhythm drifted slowly into view. They all watched for several seconds. Janet moved further back as the number of personnel and supplies of equipment increased. Sandy was standing under the archway, sobbing. Janet put her arm around the young girl.

'I can't do this job,' Sandy groaned. 'If Mr Collins dies it will be all my fault.'

'Nonsense,' Janet said firmly. 'I'm the one who should have checked on him, and I don't think he's going to die. His heart's started again now. As soon as they're happy it's going to keep going, the ambulance will get him into the emergency department and the experts will be able to take over.'

Mr Collins was being lifted onto a stretcher. Janet gave Sandy's arm a comforting squeeze. She smiled gently at the tearstained face in front of her. At thirty, Janet was only twelve years older than Sandy Smith, but right now she felt old enough to be her grandmother. 'You go and have a cup of tea and talk to Outboard for a wee while. I'll help them clear up in here.'

Janet opened the front door to allow the stretcher to be carried out. She reached down and picked up the bag of kitty litter which was still lying where Sandy had dropped it. Oliver was standing up now. He had his hand extended towards the newcomer.

'Not the ideal way to welcome even a temporary colleague,' he said dryly, 'but we're delighted to see you. I'm Oliver Spencer and that's my wife, Sophie, who's about to disappear off to hospital with Mr Collins.'

Sophie was walking beside the stretcher. She looked back and gave an apologetic wave, before heading out the door.

'I've arrived at a bad time. Might it be better if I came back later?'

'No.' Oliver shook his head firmly. 'This morning was total chaos and Mr Collins has just finished it off in style. We're in dire need of assistance.' He paused. 'You didn't tell us your name.'

No! Janet wanted to shout. Don't say it. She couldn't believe this was happening. She had never even remotely prepared herself for this possibility. She stood, frozen to the spot, blindly clutching the bag of kitty litter, using it as a shield against the confirmation she knew she couldn't avoid.

'I'm sorry,' the locum apologised. 'I thought the agency would have been in touch. I'm Dr James McFadden. Jamie,' he added as an afterthought.

Of course it was Jamie. Janet had known that the instant she'd heard the accent and tone of the once so familiar voice. The emergency had simply postponed the impact of the knowledge. Jamie McFadden. Past colleague. Past lover. The father of her twin sons. What had she told Sandy Smith so confidently? That this morning was as bad as it ever got around here?

Janet Muir had been terribly wrong.

Things had just become immeasurably worse.

CHAPTER TWO

ANY second now, Janet Muir warned herself.

The eye contact between them had all the dreadful
inevitability of a slow-motion car crash. You saw the
collision coming, knew the impact would be disas-
trous, but there wasn't a damned thing you could do
to avoid it.

Would Jamie McFadden recognise her? Would he
acknowledge the recognition? Would the memory be
as overwhelmingly gut-wrenching as that which she
was experiencing? Janet could feel the hard plastic
handle of the bag she was clutching biting into her
collar-bone. She welcomed the physical discomfort.
It was something real she could focus on in this developing nightmare.

'You're Scottish,' Oliver observed, with an amused
tilt to his mouth.

'Aye.' Jamie McFadden acknowledged the obvious
with a brief nod. His wavy hair had darkened over
the years, Janet noted. It was almost brown now.
There were enough blond streaks left to make it catch
the sunlight that streamed through the bay window of
the waiting room. It was a glorious day outside. This
really could not be happening to her.

'What part are you from?' Oliver queried.

'Glasgow,' Jamie responded. He stepped aside to

allow an ambulance officer, burdened with equipment, access to the front door.

'Really?' Oliver sounded intrigued. 'Just like Janet!'

'Sorry?' James McFadden's total lack of comprehension was evident.

'Janet Muir, our practice nurse.' Oliver's hand was coming up, ready to point her out. Jamie was turning even as Oliver finished his sentence. 'Janet's from Glasgow, too. Maybe you know each other.'

Janet didn't even attempt a smile. She knew it would have been a physical impossibility. She didn't try to speak either. She needed to concentrate on simply drawing breath. The shock in those brown eyes was startling. Janet almost felt sorry for him. She'd had several minutes since she'd recognised his voice. Several long minutes in which to try and prepare herself for this moment. Jamie had been thrown in at the deep end.

Janet's question about whether he would recognise her had been answered. Her question about the effect of the recognition was also answered. For a split second, James McFadden looked as though he'd been violently assaulted. Stabbed. Or shot. Things didn't come any more gut-wrenching than that—no matter how quickly the reaction could be shuttered.

But what of the third question? How was he going to react? Would he acknowledge her? Janet waited. Jamie was the one who had stepped—uninvited and unwanted—into her world. It was his call. If he wanted to pretend they'd never met then that was fine by her. In fact, it would be infinitely preferable to…to the warmth in Jamie McFadden's tone.

'*Janet!* I don't believe it! After all these years!' Jamie's hand was stretching towards her. Janet hugged the prickly bag of kitty litter more tightly.

'Jamie.' She tried to smile but her lips simply wouldn't co-operate. Jamie's hand faltered and then dropped to his side.

'It *was* a long time ago,' he said casually. 'Maybe you don't remember the last time we met.'

Janet stared at him. Of course she remembered. How could she possibly forget? Jamie hadn't been smiling then and his tone had been anything but warm. 'Thank God you're *not* pregnant,' he'd said coldly. 'It could never have worked.'

The awkward pause went unnoticed by Oliver as Sophie dashed back inside. 'Could you grab Mr Collins's file, please, Janet? We'll need the test results.'

'Of course.' Janet was glad of the task. She deposited her burden on the counter and swiftly located the file. Running outside, she handed it to Sophie. The back door of the ambulance slammed shut and it drove away. Janet sighed with relief. Several bystanders and a couple of afternoon clinic patients were standing outside the medical centre, staring at the ambulance and speculating in hushed conversations about the reason for its presence. The sooner they got back into some semblance of normal routine, the better.

By the time Sandy Smith returned from the staff-room, all evidence of the emergency had gone. Three patients sat, looking subdued, in a tidy waiting room. Janet had arranged the files for the scheduled afternoon appointments, switched the phone back from the answering machine and was returning the calls.

'Everything's under control,' she assured Sandy. 'Oliver should be ready for his first patient. I'll be in my room for a while. I've got to start making appointments for this week's recalls and chase up some results. Just call me if you need any help. I don't have any patients booked until 3 p.m. and they're just dry ice treatment for warts and some ear syringing.' She looked more closely at Sandy's face. 'Are you OK?'

Sandy nodded. 'I feel better now.' She lowered her voice. 'I really thought he was going to die, you know? I've never seen a dead person.' Sandy looked over the counter fearfully, as though she expected another patient to succumb. She relaxed visibly as one old lady smiled at her. 'Who's Oliver talking to in the staffroom?'

'Our new locum,' Janet answered tersely. She patted the bag of kitty litter still lying on the counter, now with the tins of cat food positioned beside it. 'Would you like to go and put these away? They're kind of in the way here.'

'Sure,' Sandy agreed as the phone started ringing. 'In a minute.' She picked up the receiver. 'Good afternoon, St David's Medical Centre. Sandy speaking.'

Janet sighed. She picked up the bag and tins herself. Why should she be intimidated into trying to hide? This was *her* territory. If anyone should feel uncomfortably unwelcome, it should be James McFadden. *She* wasn't the one who'd thrown their relationship away. *She* wasn't the one who'd had a fling with her best friend, got her pregnant and then set up house together hundreds of miles away in London. It wasn't *her* that...

The laughter coming from the staffroom suggested that Jamie was feeling anything but unwelcome.

'So you've been with St Davids for about four years, then, Oliver?' Jamie was asking.

'That's right. Janet and I started at about the same time.' Oliver smiled at Janet who nodded her confirmation of the history. She looked away quickly but Jamie hadn't taken his gaze off Oliver.

'And Josh has been here for ten?'

'And Toni,' Oliver told him. 'She started out as the receptionist when the practice was very small. She got promoted to practice manager at the same time Janet and I came here.'

'Ah.' The syllable was laced with fresh comprehension. 'You and Janet were together, then.'

Oliver laughed. 'Not in that sense, mate.'

Janet plonked the tins of cat food onto the bench. She could feel her cheeks reddening again. What was so funny about that inference? And why should Jamie McFadden sound as though he had only expected her to go somewhere with a man in tow? *He* was the one who hadn't been satisfied with a single partner.

'Oliver is married to Sophie,' she informed Jamie crisply. 'Our GP registrar.'

'But only recently, I understand.' Jamie's level gaze informed Janet that she'd had plenty of time to go in and out of a relationship with Oliver Spencer before a preferable model had shown up. The gaze

was transferred almost instantly but the message had
been clearly relayed. Janet winced at the reminder of
how easily they'd always been able to communicate.
A glance here—a touch there. It had been all that had
been necessary to convey a wealth of information.
Almost telepathy. Disturbing. Janet's hand knocked
the tin of cat food she had just put down. It rolled
into the sink with a loud clatter.

'And your senior partner, Josh, is now on honeymoon with your practice manager, Toni.' There had
been no discernible break in Jamie's observations.
Janet picked up the tin. Only telepathy could happen
that instantly.

Oliver was laughing again. 'It must be something
in the air around here. You'd better watch out, Jamie.'

Both men were looking at Janet who promptly
dropped the tin of jellymeat onto her foot and swore
effectively. Thoroughly flustered, she muttered a lame
excuse and rushed out of the staffroom. Not before
she'd heard Jamie chuckle.

'Not me, Oliver. I'm totally immune, thank God.'

She could hear the two doctors following her down
the hallway. 'This is Josh's room, Jamie. It'll be the
one you'll be using for consultations. Have a look
around. I'd better see my first patient but I'll catch
up with you again in a few minutes.'

Janet closed the door of the treatment room behind
her. She leaned against it, drawing in a deep breath.

Smoothing the skirt of her uniform against her legs,
she noticed that her hands were trembling. She took
another deep breath and let it out very slowly. Totally
immune, was he? What had happened to the great

romance between him and Sharlene? Or was he immune because he was happily married? Janet shuddered. Did she really want to find out?

No. Janet sat down at her small desk and reached for the computer printout. She unhooked the wall phone and placed it beside the list of patient names and phone numbers. Mrs Coombs was first. Her blood test had revealed severe anaemia. Oliver wanted her to come in for a series of iron injections and Janet needed to make the first appointment. She picked up the receiver and then replaced it as she heard a knock on her door. Sandy probably required some assistance.

'Come in,' Janet called cheerfully. Poor Sandy had already coped with quite enough today. Janet had no intention of letting her know how disturbed she now felt herself.

The door opened and then closed again. But it wasn't Sandy now standing close to her desk. It was Jamie McFadden.

'I get the distinct impression you're not very pleased to see me,' Jamie stated without preamble. 'Maybe it would be better if I didn't stay.'

'You have to,' Janet informed him grimly. 'We've already been let down by one locum. This is a very busy practice. Oliver can't possibly cope by himself and God knows when the agency would be able to come up with another locum.'

'He's not by himself. He has his wife working with him.'

'Sophie's a GP registrar. She's due to fly to Wellington tomorrow to sit her written exams. She'll be away for two days. She's also pregnant and suffering from severe morning sickness.'

Jamie's eyebrows lifted sardonically. 'You're right. This *is* a very busy practice.'

Janet ignored the innuendo. 'Of course, it's entirely up to you. It is somewhat of a challenge, I agree.' Her glance accused him of making a habit of running away from difficult situations. The glance was a test, given unconsciously. Did the telepathy still work both ways?

James McFadden's mouth tightened. Bingo! Janet felt suddenly calmer, as though a measure of control had landed back in her court.

'I wouldn't call it a challenge, exactly,' Jamie said thoughtfully. His gaze held Janet's firmly. 'Maybe we could see it as more of an opportunity. What happened between us would have to be considered ancient history by now. Maybe it's time to forgive and forget.' Jamie's smile was conciliatory.

'Even ancient history can leave a lasting impact on some people,' Janet said coolly. She could feel her heart pounding. Another opportunity with Jamie McFadden was the last thing she needed. The last thing she could possibly want. 'It's only for six weeks,' she said tightly. 'I'm sure we can cope.'

'But do you *want* to?'

'Yes, I do.' Janet fixed Jamie with a determined stare. 'I have an immense loyalty to this place and to these people. This is my life now, Jamie, and it's all I have. I'm not going to let some incident from my past create or add to the difficulties we're already experiencing.' Janet wished she could stand up to emphasise her determination, but even at her height of five feet seven she would still have to look a long way up to maintain eye contact with James McFadden. 'St David's is in desperate need of a locum GP. They're very difficult to come by at present and we've already lost one. I imagine the agency would tell us we're very lucky to get *you*.'

The second knock on the door was more urgent than Jamie's had been. Sandy looked agitated as she poked her head into the room without waiting for a response.

'Mrs Neville has just jammed her finger in her car door.' Sandy sounded alarmingly close to tears again. 'There's *blood* all over the place!'

Janet was on her feet instantly. She grabbed a dressings pack from the cupboard above her head without pausing. She brushed past Jamie McFadden. Mrs Neville was standing beside the reception counter. Her eyes were shut tightly and she was moaning loudly. Her uninjured hand gripped the wrist of the other. A mangled fingertip was bleeding freely onto the counter. Janet covered it with a large gauze pad and put her arm around the groaning woman supportively.

'Come with me, Mrs Neville. Let's get you sitting down and see what the damage really is.'

Somehow she wasn't surprised to find Jamie still in the treatment room. He had donned surgical gloves, poured some Betadine into a kidney bowl and opened another pack of dressings.

'Mrs Neville, is it?' he queried. His smile was professional. Reassuring. 'I'm Dr McFadden. Sit down here and show me what you've done to that poor finger.' His glance at Janet a minute later was equally professional. 'Draw up some lignocaine, will you, please, Janet? I think we'll put a nerve block in while we sort this out.' He turned back to his patient. 'It's pretty painful, isn't it?'

'Oh, yes, Doctor,' Mrs Neville gasped. 'I can't bear to look. Have I…have I cut my finger off?'

'Och, nothing like that,' Jamie assured her. 'You've squashed the top a bit, that's all. We might need to remove the nail and put a stitch or two in the back. Nothing we can't cope with.' He looked across at Janet as she held an ampoule upside down, sucking the contents out with a needle and syringe. 'Is it, Janet?'

'No, Dr McFadden.' Janet's tone was calm as she handed him the dose of local anaesthetic. She held out the empty ampoule as well so he could confirm the medication. 'Nothing we can't cope with.'

Mrs Neville looked reassured, happily oblivious to the deeper meaning of the exchange. By the time her finger was cleaned up, stitched and dressed, the middle aged patient was clearly smitten with St David's latest staff member.

'We're becoming a regular United Nations here,' she told him proudly. 'The last locum was an Indian lady and now we have you. I do love your accent.'

'You should be used to a bit of a burr.' Jamie sounded surprised. 'I understand Janet's been here for years.'

'Oh, but that's different. And your accent is so much *stronger*!'

Janet dropped the needles and the scalpel Jamie had used to tidy the edges of the wound into the sharps disposal container. Mrs Neville had been enamoured of Oliver ever since she'd started coming to St David's. Now her allegiance was clearly being transferred without difficulty. She threw a sidelong glance at the object of Mrs Neville's admiration in time to catch the cheeky, small-boy grin.

Janet closed her eyes for a split second against a wave of despair. That *grin*! She saw it a dozen times a day on the faces of her sons. She had always loved it and the two little ratbags knew it was the second best way to get around their mother. The best way, of course, were the cuddles and declarations of love. Worked a treat almost every time—especially if accompanied by *that* cheeky grin. Did she love the facial expression because she loved her sons so much? Or was it because it had subconsciously linked them to the first great love of her life?

Could she cope? How many more links might become obvious over the next six weeks? How many more reminders could she take about how she had once felt about this man? It was hard enough, listening to his voice. Mrs Neville was right. His accent was much stronger than her own. And could she keep the boys a secret? Janet shuddered at even the thought of *that* problem and turned back into Jamie's conversation. He was explaining the difference to their patient as he finished easing the finger stall over the dressing.

'I was born and raised in Glasgow,' he told Mrs Neville. 'Janet lived in Edinburgh for her formative

years. That's a much more civilised place.' Jamie's
tone suggested that civilisation was not necessarily an
attribute. 'Besides, Janet's been away from her home-
land for years. I only arrived last week.'

'Do you think you'll stay here?' Mrs Neville asked
coyly. 'Permanently, that is?'

Jamie laughed, a rich sound that caused Janet's
stomach to fold itself into an even tighter knot. 'I'm
only planning on a working holiday, Mrs Neville. I
doubt that permanence is something I'll even consider.'

Huh! Janet flashed him a meaningful glance. No.
Permanence wasn't something that would be high on
Jamie McFadden's agenda. Love them and leave
them. Jobs, countries...women. Jamie had caught the
glance. His dark brown eyes narrowed slightly as he
acknowledged the disparaging line of Janet's
thoughts. She saw a spark of anger then. Whatever
challenge he had also interpreted from her glance was
going to be risen to.

'You had an appointment with Dr Bennett, didn't
you, Mrs Neville?' Jamie's attention returned swiftly
to his patient. 'I'm afraid she's tied up at the hospital
for a while. Perhaps it's something I could help you
with?'

Mrs Neville blushed furiously. 'Oh, no! It was
nothing urgent, Dr McFadden. I'll make another appointment for later in the week.'

Janet pressed her lips together firmly as she emptied the bowl of soiled dressings and swabs into the
rubbish container. Mrs Neville had been having in-
creasing trouble with a severe case of haemorrhoids.

It had been Janet who'd suggested she see their female GP when she'd heard that the over-the-counter preparations weren't providing any relief.

'Come and see me at the same time, then,' Jamie invited. 'I'd like to check on that finger.'

Mrs Neville's gratitude at not being pressed into an explanation was patent. 'I'll do that, Dr McFadden. And thank you. Thank you *so* much! My finger doesn't hurt at all now.'

'My pleasure.' Jamie smiled. 'You'll find it gets a wee bit sore when the anaesthetic wears off, though. I'm sure Janet can give you some tablets.'

'Of course,' Janet murmured. She smiled at Mrs Neville but the woman's gaze was still firmly glued to Jamie. Oliver Spencer appeared in the doorway. He didn't appear to notice Janet either.

'At work already, Jamie? Fantastic!' He lowered his voice as Janet selected some painkillers from a nearby cupboard. 'Could I get you to see another patient? She's a fifty-four-year-old woman with a case of postherpetic neuralgia. She's in a lot of pain. She had a dose of shingles three months ago and...' Oliver's voice faded as Jamie followed him out.

Janet handed Mrs Neville the packet of tablets. 'You can take two up to every four hours,' she instructed. 'But don't take any more than that and make sure you keep your finger completely dry. I'll make an appointment for you to see Sophie on Thursday or Friday.'

'*And* Dr McFadden,' Mrs Neville reminded her firmly. She smiled rather dreamily at Janet. 'Isn't he wonderful? You're so lucky to have found him!'

'Mmm.' Janet's smile was automatic. She could hear an echo of Sharlene's voice—a bitter memory that hadn't surfaced for years. 'Oh, you're so *lucky*, Jan,' her best friend—and room-mate—had sighed. 'Where did you *find* him?'

Janet steered Mrs Neville towards the reception counter. 'Sandy will fix you up,' she said distractedly. 'Call me if you have any problems.'

The afternoon settled into a blissful period of calm. Janet found she had time to make her recall appointments as Sandy took phone calls, welcomed new arrivals and sorted out the accounts of those leaving. After the miserable chaos of the morning, Janet couldn't believe how smoothly the clinic was running. They even had time for a quick afternoon teabreak when Sophie arrived back from the hospital.

'How is Mr Collins?' Janet queried, handing Sophie a mug of coffee.

'Amazingly happy.' Sophie shook her head wonderingly. 'I left him sitting up in the coronary care unit, surrounded by monitors and shouting at a poor house surgeon.'

'What had the house surgeon done?' Oliver grinned.

'Nothing. Mr Collins lost his hearing aid somewhere between here and A and E.'

'At least he *can* shout,' Janet observed. 'I had my doubts there for a while.'

Sophie chuckled. 'Mr Collins has had an "out of body" experience. I heard all about it at least three times.'

'What—tunnels and bright lights?'

'More like kind of musical,' Sophie said thoughtfully. 'A full orchestra, he said.'

'Playing hymns?'

'No.' Sophie chuckled again. 'He said it sounded like the Crusaders' theme song. What is it? "Conquest of Paradise"?'

Janet nodded. 'Vangelis, 1492. The boys have got it on tape and it gets hammered in our house whenever there's a big rugby game coming up.'

'Anyway.' Sophie sat down with a sigh. 'Mr Collins is alive to tell the tale, thank goodness. I'm exhausted.' She looked up as Jamie McFadden entered the staffroom. 'Hi, Jamie!' Sophie's face brightened. 'I'm sorry I didn't get the chance to say hello properly. Come and sit down and have a coffee.'

'Thanks.' Jamie sat down beside Sophie. 'I'll pass on the coffee, though. I only drink tea.'

'Just like Janet!' Sophie exclaimed. 'Must be a Scottish thing.'

'That's not all that Jamie and Janet have in common,' Oliver informed his wife. 'They knew each other in Glasgow.'

Sophie's eyebrows shot up.

'We just worked together in the same hospital.' Janet placed a cup of tea in front of Jamie. 'It was a long time ago.'

'What an amazing coincidence,' Sophie breathed.

Janet frowned. It was indeed. A little too amazing. Had Jamie McFadden found out she was here somehow? Through her sister, perhaps? Liz had been planning a return to the UK at some stage. What else might he know about? Janet swallowed nervously.

'You don't take sugar, do you, Jamie?' she queried politely.

'I do, actually.' Jamie's smile was equally polite. 'But I'll get it. You sit down.' Jamie got to his feet with an easy grace and headed towards the kitchen bench. 'How did your patient get on, Sophie?' he asked over his shoulder.

'He's doing well. They were discussing the possibility of some angioplasty when I left. Mr Collins was very enthusiastic.'

'Was he?' Jamie's eyebrows rose expressively. 'Invasive interventional therapy isn't usually an attractive option.'

Oliver laughed. 'Our Mr Collins isn't a usual patient. He has a keen interest in medicine—especially when he can apply it to himself.'

'Just wait until Josh and Toni hear about this.' Sophie grinned. 'We'll have to take every complaint seriously from now on.' She shook her head. 'I'll never feel the same when I hear "Conquest of Paradise".'

Jamie looked confused.

'It's a rather stirring piece of music which our local rugby team has adopted as a theme song,' Sophie explained. 'Everybody in Christchurch—the whole of Canterbury, in fact—recognises it. Mr Collins reckons he heard it during his near-death experience.'

'Is he keen on rugby, then?' Jamie smiled.

'Most people are when Crusader fever hits town. Everybody dresses in red and black and everybody gets sick of hearing "Conquest of Paradise". There could be a big game coming up next month if they get through to the finals. You'll see what I mean then.'

'Let's hope Josh and Toni are back in time,' Oliver put in. 'Josh would hate to miss a big match.'

Jamie was adding a second spoonful of sugar to his tea. 'They're having a long honeymoon.'

'They both needed a good break.' Oliver's glance included both Sophie and Janet, who nodded their agreement. Janet was pleased to notice Jamie's expression, advertising his understanding of a bond of knowledge between the St Davids staff members that excluded the newcomer. *She* belonged here, her expression told him. *He* didn't.

Sophie was peering into her mug with distaste. 'I've gone right off coffee,' she announced. 'I think I'll switch to tea.'

'You should go home and put your feet up,' Oliver advised. 'You've had an awful day and it's an early flight tomorrow.' He looked worried. 'This exam couldn't be at a worse time for you. Maybe you should ask for a postponement.'

'No way!' Sophie decared. 'All that swotting for nothing? I'll be fine, Oliver—as long as there's a toilet nearby. I wouldn't mind heading home now, though. Do you think you can cope without me?'

'Jamie's doing a fantastic job already,' Oliver informed his wife. Jamie shrugged modestly.

'You've got a great set-up here,' he complimented Oliver. 'Your record-keeping is superb and you and Janet have been very helpful with my queries regarding prescriptions and so on.'

Oliver and Sophie exchanged glances. Then Oliver

got to his feet. 'I haven't given you a proper tour of the place yet. Let's do it while we've got a quiet spell. You'd better see where we keep the life pack and the oxygen and so on.'

Jamie nodded. 'After your Mr Collins, I think that would be a very good idea.'

'That sort of thing doesn't happen very often.' Oliver smiled. 'Don't expect too much excitement at St David's.'

'Och, I don't.' Jamie's gaze landed on Janet. 'But life has a way of throwing a few surprises at you.'

Sophie hadn't failed to notice the direction of Jamie's comment. 'It has, indeed,' she agreed happily. 'Good luck for the next couple of days, Jamie. I'll look forward to seeing you again when I'm back from Wellington.'

Sophie barely contained herself until the men left the room. She nudged Janet meaningfully. 'Not bad. You must be looking forward to a chance to catch up.' She wiggled her eyebrows. 'Or reminisce, maybe?'

Janet rolled her eyes. 'Give me a break.' She ignored Sophie's hopeful expression. 'Oliver's right, Sophie. You'd better go home and have a rest.' She picked up the empty mugs the men had left on the table. 'And I'd better get on. I've got some warts waiting to be done.' Turning back to collect Sophie's abandoned mug of coffee, Janet chewed her lip for a moment. 'Sophie?'

'Mmm?'

'Could you ask Oliver...? I mean, could you and Oliver...?' Janet paused uncomfortably.

'Could we what, Janet?' Sophie frowned in concern. 'Are you worried about something?'

'It's just…' Janet busied herself with the mugs. 'I'd rather that Jamie McFadden didn't find out about the twins.' *That* was the understatement of the century! Janet glanced over her shoulder to see whether Sophie had read anything more into her attempt at a casual request.

She had. But not what Janet had feared. Sophie's smile was understanding. The gleam in her eyes was knowing. 'My lips are sealed,' she promised. 'And I'll make sure Oliver's are as well.' She smiled broadly at Janet. 'They *have* been known to complicate things in that direction, haven't they?'

'Mmm.' Janet was wondering desperately whether correcting Sophie's erroneous assumption would complicate matters even more.

'What was it they called your last boyfriend? A dork?' Sophie giggled. 'Dennis the dork. No wonder he took off! Don't worry.' Sophie tapped the side of her nose. 'As far as Dr Jamie McFadden will know, you're single and unencumbered. It'll be entirely up to you when you tell him.'

'Thanks.' Janet smiled tightly. She had no intention whatsoever of telling James McFadden about her children. It would be a disaster if he found out the truth and it was a disaster that Janet Muir was determined wouldn't occur.

CHAPTER THREE

'WHAT'S for tea, Mum?'

'Bread and water,' Janet told Adam sternly. She opened the back door of her small car and closed her eyes to the large clod that dropped from Adam's shoe to be trodden into the carpet by Rory as he bounced into the back seat beside his brother.

Rory's grin reassured Adam that he didn't need to believe Janet's threat of culinary punishment. Adam still looked worried.

'Put your seat belts on,' Janet ordered as she slid behind the steering-wheel. 'Mrs Carpenter told me you were late again today.'

There was a short silence from the back seat. Mrs Carpenter lived only three doors away from their school. As the ideal position for an after-school caregiver, Enid Carpenter's address had been a large deciding factor when Janet had chosen the older woman to care for the twins between 3 and 5 p.m. on weekdays. Along with the lower than average cost of five dollars an hour and Mrs Carpenter's availability to care for the boys in the holidays and at home on the odd occasion when they'd been too sick to go to school.

It was an arrangement which had apparently worked well over the last eighteen months but recently Janet had detected less willingness on Enid

Carpenter's part. Janet sighed, slowing down for the roundabout near the shopping centre. The twins were becoming more of a handful for everybody, including herself, and she worried constantly about the level of supervision they actually received after school. Enid provided afternoon tea and was supposed to encourage homework. She was more likely to give the boys free run of her garden or unlimited television when the weather was wet. Janet wasn't about to rush into criticising the caregiver, however. If Mrs Carpenter threw in the towel the boys would have to go to the same kind of day care facility she had used when they were toddlers and that would cost far more than she could afford. The early years had depleted her life savings to an alarmingly low level.

'It shouldn't take you more than five minutes to get to Mrs Carpenter's house after school,' Janet reminded the boys sharply. 'She said it was nearly 4 o'clock when you arrived. She'd been about to go looking for you.' And that was another worry. Janet would have been out looking for the twins within minutes of their non-arrival. Did Enid Carpenter really care about her sons?

'We had to stay in after school,' Adam confessed.

'Why?'

'To pick up all the maths counters,' Rory explained.

'There were an awful lot,' Adam added sadly. 'It took a long time.'

'Why did you have to pick them all up?' Janet was sure she already knew the answer but the inquisition was a ritual that needed to be gone through.

There was another short silence, broken by a mutter from Adam. 'Because we threw them.'

'Ah!' Janet murmured significantly.

'It wasn't just us, Mum,' Rory protested. 'John and Michael and Ben were throwing them at the girls, too.'

'And did John and Michael and Ben have to stay in after school and pick them up?'

'No.' Both twins sounded indignant.

'Why not?'

'They said we started it.'

'And did you?'

'No,' Rory stated emphatically. 'It was the girls that started it.'

'Yeah!' Adam supported his brother. 'They called us clones.'

Janet looked in her rear-view mirror. Two identical little faces could be seen. Two identical mops of blond curls, four dark brown eyes. Two matching injured expressions.

'We didn't hit them this time,' Adam said virtuously. 'That was good, wasn't it, Mum?'

'Yes.' Janet smothered a smile. 'But you shouldn't have started throwing counters either.' Another glance in the mirror revealed the silent communication between the six-year-olds. The trouble they'd brought on themselves had been well worth it. Janet sighed again.

'What's *really* for tea, Mum?'

'Sausages.'

'Cool! And chips?' The boys spoke in unison. A common enough event. Janet had often wondered whether they had some sort of telepathic connection. Like she had...with their father.

'No.' Janet's clipped tone brooked no protest. 'Mashed potatoes.' She turned the car into the overgrown driveway and parked under a carport, the roof of which was only a memory. 'Take your shoes off *before* you go inside,' she added warningly. 'And then it's time for homework.'

The boys were fighting over the only available pencil within five minutes. Janet was shovelling the cold ashes from the fire into the bucket. It may have been a lovely day but this living room seemed to stay damp and cold in the evenings until midsummer. It was too soon to give up the daily ritual of lighting the fire. 'Cut it out!' she warned the twins. 'I don't want to hear any more arguments.'

There were the sounds of a continued scuffle then an anguished wail.

'Adam broke the pencil, Mum! And it was *mine*!'

'It wasn't!' Adam yelled. 'It was *mine*!'

'I don't care whose it was,' Janet snapped. 'I'm fed up with you two fighting.' She put the bucket down with a bang. A cloud of coal dust drifted up and clung to the skirt of her uniform. Janet brushed at it with her hand, turning the dust into grimy streaks. It was only then that she remembered about the washing machine.

'Oh, God!' Janet groaned. The combined disasters of the day rushed at her like a tidal wave. She could feel tears threatening as the stress of a hard day at work and the emotional nightmare of James McFadden stepping back into her life hit home. And now her children were misbehaving, her only uniform was filthy and she had no way of cleaning it.

'What's wrong, Mummy?' Two small arms were coming around her from one side.

'Don't cry!' Two more arms came from the other side.

'We're sorry,' Adam announced. 'We won't fight any more.'

'We'll share the pencil,' Rory suggested brightly. 'I can sharpen both ends with the Swiss army knife that Josh gave me.'

Janet drew the twins close. 'It's not that,' she explained, trying to steady her voice. 'I've just had a bad day and I'm a bit tired. And I've got an awful lot of washing to do and I forgot to get someone to come and fix the washing machine for me.'

'I think I know what's wrong with the washing machine.'

Janet sniffed and looked at Rory a trifle suspiciously. 'How would you know that, Rory?'

'Well, when Adam and I were playing marbles yesterday, one of my best ones—you know the one with the green and pink blobby bits inside?'

'Mmm.' Janet nodded. 'What about it?'

'Well, it went behind the washing machine.'

'And?'

'And I got the broom handle and poked it out.'

'Why would that make the washing machine leak?'

'The stick got stuck on the hose thing,' Adam offered. 'And it kind of fell off.'

'Why didn't you tell me about that this morning?'

'Because you'd be cross.'

Janet looked down at the matching, repentant faces. If the twins had had blue eyes they would have looked like choir boys. A pair of angels. Instead, they'd inherited their father's brown eyes—and the temperaments of little devils.

'We love you, Mum,' the boys chorused, playing their trump card. 'We'll fix the washing machine.'

'No. I'll do it,' Janet said firmly. 'Thank you for telling me. But even if I do fix it and get the washing done, I can't get it dry by the morning. You'll have to wear shorts to school tomorrow.'

'You could light the fire.' Rory always had the imaginative ideas. 'And dry things on the fence.' He pointed to the fire guard.

'We could bring in some wood,' Adam suggested, always the more practical.

'That's a great idea.' Janet gave the boys another squeeze. 'You do that while I see about the washing machine and getting tea ready. Then I'll help you with your homework after your bath.' She halted the headlong rush towards the back door with a firm command. 'Put your gumboots on before you go out to the woodshed and take them *off* before you come back inside.'

Somehow the chores got done. Even the painfully slow process of encouraging the boys to attempt their detested reading homework. Essential items of clothing for the morning, including Janet's uniform, were draped, steaming quietly, over the fire guard. The twins were in their bunk beds, sound asleep. One of the more redeeming features of their full-tilt, find-as-much-trouble-as-possible attitude to life was that they tended to fall asleep the instant their curly blond heads hit their pillows.

For the first time since six that morning, Janet could sit down without the pressure of endless, urgent tasks taking any pleasure away from the break. The dishes could wait. The ironing would have to wait. She could sit in the old armchair which her sister, Liz, had found in a garage sale years ago and watch the washing dry.

Bliss! Janet closed her eyes to enjoy the sensation of peace more thoroughly. A minute later, she was staring at the washing again, a frown creasing her forehead. Relatively speaking, this was perfectly peaceful. As peaceful as the real world allowed for single mothers. But Janet Muir knew what perfect peace actually was.

She had known it—just once—and the memory was as clear as it was disturbing. It wasn't disturbing because she wanted it again. Far from it. Perfection couldn't exist in the real world and it was better not to find it by stepping aside from reality. When you did find it, the promise it gave couldn't be honoured. The only outcome could be betrayal and pain.

But hadn't it been worth it? That time away from time? The vision of what joy human existence could aspire to? The insight into what a relationship between a man and a woman could actually be? Janet closed her eyes again with a long, long sigh. She could almost feel the same prickle of excitement which the prospect of precisely that period of time had evoked...

The excitement of finally having some time alone

together. Janet Muir had been twenty-two years old, working as a newly qualified nurse in Glasgow's Western Infirmary. Jamie McFadden had been twenty-seven, in his second year on the wards. They'd met the day Janet had started duties in the general surgical ward. The attraction had been instantaneous—and mutual. The first date had been within days—a drink at the local pub, followed by fish dinners which they'd eaten out of the paper bags while sitting on the steps of the nurses' home. Janet's 10 p.m. curfew and the conversation neither had wanted to curtail at the pub had left no time for anything more glamorous.

That first date had been two months ago, and both Jamie and Janet had been increasingly desperate to get closer. It had been hard enough to find time to be together. Janet's shifts had been disruptive and Jamie's schedule a punishing one. It had been totally impossible to find privacy. Both of them had been living in at the infirmary. Both had had room-mates sharing their cramped quarters. The coincidence of having two days off at the same time had been too good an opportunity to miss. Jamie had persuaded his room-mate to lend them his car. He had been waiting out on the street with the engine running and the passenger door open for Janet when she'd run out, an overnight bag clutched in one hand, an excited grin lighting her face.

'Where shall we go?' Jamie asked. 'You choose.'

'No, you choose.' Janet laughed. 'I don't care. I'll go anywhere with you, Jamie McFadden. All the way.'

'Be careful,' he warned. 'I might take you up on that.'

They both laughed but the long glance they shared was much more serious. This opportunity was what they had both longed for. They both knew it was only a beginning. Having finally won the time together, the urgency seemed to evaporate. They drove north out of Glasgow on the A82 until they reached Crianlarich. Janet studied the signpost.

'Let's take the A85 to Oban,' she suggested.

At Oban, neither Janet nor Jamie felt inclined to stop the journey which had become a pleasure in itself, prolonging the anticipation of what lay at the end. They took the ferry across to the island of Mull. At the end of the wharf was another signpost, the arm pointing to the right indicating the main town of Tobermory. The left hand arm simply said 'Iona Ferry'.

'Funny name for a town,' Jamie mused. 'Which way shall we go, Janna? You choose.'

'No, you choose.'

Laughing, they spoke in unison. 'Let's toss a coin.' Laughing even more, they managed the feat again. 'Tails for Tobermory!'

The coin showed heads. They drove to Iona Ferry and discovered they would have to abandon the car. The ferry was, indeed, a boat and no cars were allowed on the tiny island of Iona. Being mid-week, they had no trouble securing a room at the hotel. A reduced rate was offered on the best room in the establishment—upstairs, with a sea view from the double bed.

It was only twenty-four hours from when they arrived until they had to leave the island. It was twenty-four hours that Janet would never forget. The island was bare and windswept, famous for being the first site for the introduction of Christianity to Scotland, with the arrival of St Columba in AD563. Jamie and Janet explored the abbey and St Oran's chapel, admired the Celtic crosses and marvelled over the history, with fifty Scottish kings buried in the cemetery.

The magic of the place was more than its isolation and history could account for. There was a detachment and peace that encompassed the visitors from the moment they set foot on the shore. The magic touched the first love-making of Janet Muir and Jamie McFadden. It could have been a ritual that had been pre-ordained. There was no need for haste, and passion only added to the reverence with which they welcomed the discovery of their love. A love that was now complete on all levels.

It was the faint smell of singeing that roused Janet from the melancholy the memory left her with. She brushed the tears from her cheeks with irritation.

'You got over that years ago,' she reminded herself harshly. 'There's no reason to dredge it all up again.'

Except now there was every reason, thanks to Jamie McFadden. *Why* had he come here? It was too awful a prospect to consider that he might have come looking for her. If she was going to cope with this at all she would have to assume it was simply a bad card in the hand fate had dealt. It was only temporary and she'd told Jamie she could cope. Janet had coped with a great deal over the last seven and a half years. She was an expert.

Her expertise in coping with her sons was called on heavily the following morning and it was harder than usual, thanks to her late night and a very poor sleep.

'Why can't we have Pop Tarts for breakfast?' Adam demanded.

'Turn your T-shirt out the right way,' Janet instructed. 'And brush your hair. Rory, where are your shoes?'

'I can't find them.'

'They were on the back step last night.' Janet frowned at Adam who stamped out of the kitchen to attend to his hair. She turned back to Rory. 'Have you looked for your shoes?'

'Yes. Why can't we have Fruity Loops for breakfast?'

'Because you're having porridge.'

'Porridge sucks.'

'Mum!' Adam wailed from upstairs. 'Where's my hairbrush?'

'Where you left it,' Janet shouted back. 'Hurry up. Breakfast is ready.'

The boys sat down reluctantly at the small kitchen table. Three bowls of porridge steamed vigorously and sat untouched, like a scene from *Goldilocks and the Three Bears*.

'Ben's rat has had babies,' Rory informed Janet.

'Mmm.' Janet tried to sound enthusiastic. 'Eat up. It's nearly time to go.'

The twins both reached for the sugar bowl at the

same time. The resultant scuffle left a sticky layer of brown sugar over the table. Janet intervened when they both lunged for the milk bottle. She poured it herself.

'That's too much milk,' Rory said disgustedly. 'Yuck!'

'Ben said we could have a baby rat, Mum.' Adam took a mouthful of his porridge.

'Did he?' Janet had finished her breakfast. She put the bowl into the sink and began to wipe the sugar from the table top.

'Can we?'

'No.' Janet moved back to the bench and started sorting out the lunch box supplies. The sandwiches had been made last night when the ironing had been completed.

'Can we have a dog instead, then?'

'No.' Janet added fruit and muesli bars to the boxes.

'Why can't we buy lunch?' Adam asked petulantly.

Janet sighed. This was a routine they went through every second day. Why couldn't the boys discover it was boring on top of being ineffective? 'Because it's too expensive.'

'Ben has fish and chips every day.'

'Ben will get fat, have a lot of pimples and end up with early heart disease.' Janet glanced at the boys. Rory was making roads with his spoon through his half-eaten porridge. She removed the bowls. 'Go and wash your faces and clean your teeth. Make sure your homework books are in your bags. And, Rory—*find* your shoes. We're leaving in two minutes.'

It took five minutes to find the shoes, which Janet discovered sitting on the back step in full view. It took another five to get the boys into the car. They ran through the school gates just as the bell was ringing and Janet was five minutes late for her 9 a.m. start at St David's.

Outboard was sitting on the reception counter, surveying the mercifully empty waiting room. Sandy Smith smiled brightly.

'Morning, Janet.'

'Morning, Sandy. Have you recovered from yesterday?'

Sandy rolled her eyes. 'I think so. I hope today's a bit quieter.'

'Bound to be.' Janet wasn't going to tempt fate again. 'Is Oliver here yet?'

'Yes. He's in the staffroom with Jamie.' Sandy looked away but Janet detected a faint rise in her colour as she mentioned their locum's name. Janet's heart sank. That was all she needed. A smitten eighteen-year-old reminding her of how she'd felt when she'd first met Jamie McFadden. How even mentioning his name had quickened her pulse rate and made it difficult to concentrate on whatever task she'd been assigned. Thank goodness she didn't have to cope with feeling attracted to the man any more.

Hearing the rich sound of his brogue moments later, Janet dismissed the skip of her pulse as trepidation. She carried on to the staffroom resolutely.

'Morning, Jamie. Morning, Oliver. How was Sophie this morning?'

'Not too bad. Still throwing up. She's going to ask

the air hostess for a supply of those paper bags to take to the exams.'

'Poor thing.' Janet opened the refrigerator to put away the yoghurt she'd brought for her lunch. At the periphery of her vision she could see Jamie sitting at the table. His body posture was relaxed, his hands idly mangling the tubing of a stethoscope. Janet shut the fridge door firmly enough to make the contents rattle. How on earth could just the sight of a man's hands be responsible for a wave of sensation that felt horribly like physical attraction? Because she knew those particular hands and what they were capable of doing to her body? *Had* been capable of doing, Janet reminded herself grimly. Past tense. The only emotion their presence should evoke now was embarrassment. And maybe that's what it was. That would explain why her cheeks felt so warm.

'All quiet on the Western Front?' Oliver queried.

'So far.' Janet nodded politely at Jamie. 'Maybe you'll get an idea of a more normal day at St David's today.'

'I'll cope,' Jamie responded. His smile was bland. 'I'm ready for anything after yesterday.' The intense scrutiny he was subjecting Janet to belied his casual tone and smile. Janet drew in a quick breath. Was that a challenge she was receiving? Or an invitation? Oliver had noticed an undercurrent as well. Unseen by Jamie, he winked at Janet, who almost groaned aloud. Instead, she raised her eyebrows questioningly.

'What time slot do you want set aside for repeat prescriptions today, Oliver?'

'Make it 11.30. If there are any house calls needed

I'll do them at lunchtime.' Oliver turned to Jamie.
'We don't charge patients for an appointment when
they just need a repeat but we like to do a quick check
and have a chat to make sure there are no problems
with side effects and so on. We can generally fit in
as many as are needed in half an hour.'

'Are house calls standard practice?'

'No. Only emergencies or our rest home and ter-
minally ill patients.'

'I'll need a good map if you want to send me out.
I'm hopeless at navigating.'

'Just toss a coin at the intersections.' Janet was
horrified when the suggestion popped out. Jamie's
glance in her direction was instantaneous and intense.
What was she trying to do? Stir up old memories and
make things even *more* difficult? Oliver hadn't noticed anything untoward.

'Don't worry,' he reassured Jamie. 'If you do need
to go out you can take Janet with you.'

That'll be the day, Janet thought fiercely. She'd run
a mile before she sat in a car alone with Jamie
McFadden. She had every intention of avoiding even
being alone in a room with him if possible. Thank
goodness for the patients. Janet's morning began quietly but quickly picked up momentum.

Mrs Crowe's diabetic ulcer needed dressing. She
was also due for her six monthly check of weight,
blood pressure, pedal pulses and eyes. It was Jamie
who popped in to conduct the examination with an
ophthalmoscope.

'Have you done the Snellen chart?' he asked Janet.

'Of course. There's actually been an improvement since Mrs Crowe's last test.'

'New glasses,' their patient explained. 'They're wonderful.'

Jamie smiled at Mrs Crowe. 'Makes a difference, doesn't it? Can you take them off for a wee minute? I just want to shine this bright light in your eyes and check that your diabetes isn't affecting the blood vessels. Look straight ahead and fix your eyes on an object. Try not to blink.'

Jamie leaned close, steadying Mrs Crowe's head with one hand. The ophthalmoscope was held against his own eye and he moved his head and the instrument together as though fused into a single piece of equipment. Janet could sense his level of concentration and couldn't resist the opportunity to study his face.

It was a very Glaswegian face. Rather craggy, with strong features and almost harsh lines. A menacing face when angry. It was the humour in those brown eyes and the mobility of his mouth that brought Jamie's face to life and made it so attractive. There were more lines around his eyes now, and a furrow on his brow that suggested frowns had become nearly as familiar as the smiles she remembered. Had life hardened Jamie McFadden and chased some of the humour away? Jamie looked up suddenly and Janet flinched, caught out in her scrutiny.

'Mrs Crowe's eyes look fine,' he reported. 'I'll make a note on her file. Are you taking any bloods?'

'Yes. We're watching Mrs Crowe's cholesterol level carefully at present.'

'Good.' Jamie straightened, handing the ophthalmoscope to Janet. 'That's you, then, Mrs Crowe.' He nodded at his patient, before catching Janet's gaze again. This time she was ready. 'Anything else you need me for at the moment?'

'No.' Janet held the gaze. 'Absolutely nothing.'

Fortunately, that remained the case for the rest of the morning. Janet saw Mrs Terence who needed a new supply of nicotine replacement patches and encouragement in her smoking cessation programme. She syringed old Mr Shaw's ears, took blood to measure the digoxin levels in Brian Talley's blood, resterilised all the minor surgery equipment and spent some time on the phone, chasing down a twelve-month-old CT scan result that Oliver wanted for a new patient.

Oliver went out to make a house call during the lunch-break and Janet ate her yoghurt quickly, knowing that Jamie was still seeing a patient. She would look after the front office while Sandy had a break and hopefully she would avoid any time alone with Jamie. Making a cup of tea to take with her, Janet was interrupted by the phone call Sandy redirected to the staffroom.

'Hullo, Madeleine.' Janet was on first-name terms with the headmistress of the boys' school. The amount of contact they'd had since the twins had begun their education meant they knew each other rather well. Janet's heart sank as Madeleine Banes spoke. She recognised a major issue when it was broached. What had the boys been up to now?

'Have you got time to come down to school for a chat today?' Miss Banes asked casually.

Janet observed Jamie's entry to the staffroom with some dismay. She could hardly request time off to visit the local primary school for half an hour without Jamie wondering what her involvement might be.

'It's a little difficult today, Madeleine,' Janet said apologetically. 'What's the problem exactly?'

'It's the boys' reading,' Madeleine explained. 'Their teacher's just done some testing and she's rather worried. I mentioned a reading recovery programme to you a while back. I think we need to get the boys some specialist help but I don't want you to get alarmed about it. That's why I thought we should have a chat.'

'How serious do you think it is?' Janet stepped to one side of the bench as Jamie reached for a teabag and a mug. At least it sounded as if she could be discussing a medical condition.

'The basic skills are in place, such as handling books, using visual clues and left-to-right eye movement. It's the basic vocabulary and initial consonant skills that are a problem. And the comprehension.'

'Ah.' Janet tried to sound professionally detached. 'That does sound like a problem.'

'It's not that they're at all slow,' Madeleine continued. 'If anything, they're too bright. They can't be bothered trying to work out what a word actually is so they just make up substitutes. They can rattle off a story in no time flat.' Miss Banes laughed. 'The ones they come up with are often better than the original. Especially Rory's. He's very imaginative.'

'Mmm.' Janet watched Jamie add sugar to his tea. He cast a sidelong glance at her, then moved to the table, picking up a copy of the *GP Weekly*.

'Unfortunately, it's not reading,' Miss Banes said sadly.

'No.' Janet wanted to wind the conversation up. She felt nervous, having Jamie so close. 'I think you're absolutely right, Madeleine. Some specialist attention *is* called for.' There. That sounded very medical. 'Is there anything else you need from me at present?'

'Ah…' The headmistress sounded faintly puzzled. 'Well, once the programme is under way we'd like to get you involved. Reinforcement at home is vital.'

'Of course,' Janet agreed. 'I'm more than happy to do that. It's not a field I've had much experience in, though.'

'A lot of it is just showing interest and providing encouragement,' Madeleine said warmly. 'You're a great mother, Janet. You do that by instinct anyway. I know it's not easy, being a single parent, and you've got quite a handful there.'

'Thanks. It's nice to get the encouragement myself. Thanks for calling, Madeleine. I'll look forward to hearing how things go.' Janet finished the call, congratulating herself on failing to arouse any suspicions in Jamie. Perhaps keeping the children a secret would be easier than she'd feared.

Her confidence lasted until after 4 p.m. The after-school rush kept them all busy, with ear and throat infections being the order of the day for the doctors.

Janet was labelling another throat-swab sample when Jamie entered the treatment room.

'I need the tympanometer again,' he told her.

'It's over there beside the autoclave.' Janet put the plastic tube holding the swab into a sample bag and sealed it.

'No, it's not.'

'Oh.' Janet looked around the room. 'It must be here somewhere, unless Oliver took it when I wasn't looking.'

Sandy Smith appeared in the doorway. She was advertising some urgency with her message. 'Mrs Carpenter's on the phone,' she told Janet anxiously. 'She says the boys have just burnt down her garden shed and could you please come and take them home?'

Janet gasped. 'Are they hurt?'

'She says they're fine. There's a policeman talking to them. They'd like to talk to you as well.'

'Tell her I'll be there in ten minutes.' Janet quickly scribbled on the sample bag and stapled the request form to the top. As Sandy scurried away, Janet became aware of the stunned immobility of the man standing nearby.

'The *boys*?' Jamie pronounced incredulously. 'You have *children*?'

'Yes.' Janet flashed him a defensive glance. There was no point in trying to keep them a secret now, but there was no way Jamie McFadden was going to find out the whole truth. 'I have two boys.'

'*Two?*'

Janet was rapidly clearing her bench. 'Last time I counted,' she agreed casually.

'And who's Mrs Carpenter?'

'The babysitter,' Janet informed him tightly. She could see what he thought of her mothering skills. No need for telepathy here—it was written all over his face. And no wonder. Had burning the shed down been an accident...or arson? Janet turned to leave but found her arm gripped. She tried to shake free. Jamie McFadden had no right to touch her. She could feel the intensity in the vice-like grip and met Jamie's stare defiantly—daring him to ask any more personal questions. He did.

'You're still using your maiden name. How was I supposed to know you were married?'

'I'm not,' Janet snapped. 'Being unmarried is hardly an effective contraceptive, unfortunately.'

'Bit careless, letting it happen *twice*,' Jamie said incredulously. 'How old are these boys?'

'Five.' The lie was actually quite difficult to get past her lips. Janet found herself succumbing to the childish gesture of putting her free arm behind her back and crossing her fingers. 'Nearly six,' she added, for good measure.

'What—*both* of them?'

'They're twins.' Janet's tone became sarcastic. 'You know, when two babies are born at the same time?'

She could see the rapid calculations going on in Jamie's brain as he slowly released his hold on her arm. As long as he believed the ages she'd given, he couldn't possibly associate these children with himself.

'What about their *father*?' Jamie still sounded stunned.

Janet rubbed at her arm. She could still feel the imprint of Jamie's fingers. Then she turned away abruptly, reaching for the bag she'd tucked under her desk. 'Their father was never interested and will never have anything to do with them. I've managed fine so far.'

'Sounds like it,' Jamie murmured. 'Do they often burn down buildings when you're not looking?'

'This is none of your business, Jamie.' Janet kept her voice low, her eye on the treatment-room door. 'Nothing to do with me is any of your business,' she added vehemently. 'You're here for six weeks and then you'll disappear from my life—again. The less we have to do with each other in the meantime, the better.'

CHAPTER FOUR

THE silence around the dinner table was oppressive.

The reheated, leftover sausages were unappealing despite the gravy Janet had used to disguise them. No wonder the twins were eating as slowly as humanly possible. Janet put down her own fork.

'How *could* you?' she asked again sadly. 'How could you *do* it?'

'We didn't mean to, Mum.' Adam's wide brown eyes filled with tears. 'It was an accident. We were just playing with the magnifying glass and the paper.'

'You let us do it,' Rory reminded her. 'When we burnt the edges of those treasure maps we made.'

'Yes, but we did it outside.' Janet sighed. 'Not in a shed full of flammable things. And you had adult supervision.'

'Mrs Carpenter never comes outside with us. She tells us to go and amuse ourselves 'cos she's busy.'

'Mrs Carpenter won't be looking after you any more.' Janet stared at her plate. 'I don't know what we're going to do.'

'We could walk down to find you after school,' Rory suggested. 'It's not very far and I know the way.'

'I can't have you at the clinic for hours every day.' Janet shook her head firmly. 'I can't watch you when I'm supposed to be working.'

'We'd be good,' Adam promised. 'And Josh lets us use his computer sometimes.'

'Yeah!' Rory's face lightened for the first time since the lecture the young policeman had delivered. 'Cool!'

'No,' Janet said sharply. The computer was in Josh's office. The office Jamie McFadden was currently occupying. Imagine what would happen if Jamie's suspicions of the twins' paternity were aroused by close contact. They might be small enough for their age to pass for being a year younger than they actually were, but that was one risk too many. The nightmare was worsening, and fear made Janet angry. 'What's more, you won't be getting your own computer for your birthday any more. It took me a year to save enough for the deposit and now I'm going to have to give it all to Mrs Carpenter to pay for the shed.'

Adam burst into tears. Rory looked anguished. Janet looked at them both and felt her own anger give way to despair. She wanted so much for her boys. She had fought so hard for the independence of her tiny family and here they were—all utterly miserable. Janet covered her eyes with her hand, struggling for control.

'It's all right, Mum,' Rory said bravely. 'We don't mind…about the computer. We still love you.'

Janet's sob turned into a laugh. Her chair scraped noisily on the wooden floorboards as she pushed it back and held out her arms. Both boys rushed to lay first claim to her lap. She managed to fit them both on. The love she felt for these children overrode her despair. Somehow she would cope. She would sort out the help she needed with their after-school care, become involved with helping with their reading difficulties and maybe even find a way to spend more time with them. She kissed the top of Adam's head, snuggled under her right-collar bone, then she turned her head to the left and kissed Rory's curls.

'It'll be OK,' she murmured. 'I'll sort everything out. We'll manage.' She gave them both a squeeze. 'What say we forget the sausages and go and get some fish and chips?'

Her lap was emptied instantaneously. Both boys gazed at her adoringly. 'Cool!' they chorused.

Janet put the screwed-up wrapping paper from their substitute dinner into the rubbish bin after the twins had gone to bed. She eyed the now congealed plates of sausages and gravy sitting on the bench. The thought occurred to her that it would be quite useful to have a dog in residence. The boys would be in heaven if they got a puppy for their birthday. They wouldn't even miss the promised computer. But how could she care for a dog when she was working all day? And what about the expense? It wasn't just the food. There were all the accessories and the registration and probably vet bills. Look at Outboard. It had cost Josh three hundred dollars to have the kitten's broken leg operated on after he'd nearly run over the abandoned animal.

It all came down to finances in the end. If she didn't have to work then she would have all the time in the world to spend with her sons. Surely there was a compromise to be found? Janet ran hot water into the kitchen sink and added detergent. If she could cut down her hours at St David's she could be home for the boys after school. If she didn't have to pay Mrs Carpenter it might make up for the cut in her wages. Janet felt a ray of hope. It wasn't the best time to make changes in the running of the clinic, with the senior partner and the practice manager away, but Oliver Spencer was very approachable and Janet desperately needed some help.

Oliver was more than approachable. Janet had waited until after lunch for a private conversation in his office. 'I think it's a great idea,' he enthused. 'A family has to come first.' He smiled somewhat proudly and Janet was reminded of his own impending fatherhood. 'In fact, we could look at employing a second nurse part time and you could cut back to just mornings.'

'Oh, no,' Janet demurred hurriedly. 'I couldn't afford that. If I just stop an hour or so earlier it should work. By the time the boys organise themselves and walk here after school, it'll be nearly 3.30 p.m. They can sit in the waiting room while I tidy up. They've sworn they'll behave. I'll work through my lunchbreak to make up some of the time.'

'No, don't do that,' Oliver protested. 'We'll manage. Don't worry.'

'It's just such a bad time for all this,' Janet apologised. 'I mean, I'm thrilled to bits that Josh and Toni got married but their honeymoon is turning into a bit of a disaster as far as St David's is concerned.'

'I haven't helped.' Oliver grinned. 'I have to take responsibility for getting Sophie pregnant.'

'Have you heard from her?'

'She rang last night. The first day went very well as far as the exams went. She's still feeling as sick as a dog. I'm going to collect her from the airport this evening.'

'She'll be exhausted,' Janet sympathised. 'Maybe she'd better stay home tomorrow.'

'Maybe.' Oliver looked worried but then brightened. 'At least we have Jamie,' he said happily. 'He's fitting in very well, and from what I've seen he's an excellent doctor. I really like him,' he added more quietly.

'That's good.' Janet ignored the questioning expression with which Oliver was inviting a more personal response. She summoned a smile. 'I've got Pagan Ellis waiting to see me. I'll ask her what she thinks of Jamie's aura.'

'And I've got a quick call to go to at the Bay Villa Rest Home. Muriel Stafford fell out of bed in the night. Sounds like she might have broken her hip.'

Pagan Ellis was looking enormous. The bulge of her advancing pregnancy was enhanced by the flowing long dress she wore.

'Not long to go now.' Janet smiled. 'How are you feeling?'

'Wonderful!' Pagan's bangles clinked as she waved her arms enthusiastically. 'Couldn't be better. I'm wondering why I ever agreed to have the baby in hospital now. With weather like this I just want to head for the beach.'

Janet shook her head warningly. 'Please, Pagan. No more of the birth in the surf plan. That premature labour when you had the flu gave us all enough of a fright.'

'It didn't come to anything, though.' Pagan smiled with satisfaction. 'Everything's back on track. The planets are on my side. Fifteen days to go.'

'Have you done your urine sample?' Janet ushered Pagan towards the scales in the treatment room. Pagan handed over a container as she climbed onto the scales.

'I'm the size of a house!' she announced proudly. 'Look at that! I've put on four kilos since last week.'

'Hmm.' Janet pointed to the chair at the end of the bed. 'Have a seat, Pagan. I'll just test your urine before I take your blood pressure.'

The dip-stick test was done quickly. The result was disconcerting, especially in conjunction with Pagan's dramatic weight gain. Protein in the urine signified abnormal kidney function. Janet wrapped the blood-pressure cuff around Pagan's upper arm.

'Have you noticed any puffiness around your eyes or neck? Or swelling of your feet and ankles? Or your hands?'

'Look at that!' Pagan held out her hands. The numerous silver rings were cutting deeply into her fingers. 'It's just normal, isn't it? Part of getting fatter?'

'It may not be,' Janet said cautiously. 'Rest your hand in your lap while I take this pressure.' Janet was silent for a minute as she concentrated. She frowned as she repeated the test. 'Your blood pressure's up a bit, too,' she told Pagan. 'When are you due to see the specialist again?'

'Next Monday.'

'I'll see if Dr Spencer's back from his house call,' Janet decided. 'I'd like him to have a look at you.'

'No.' Pagan shook her head. 'I only see Sophie.'

'She's away today. She's sitting her exams in Wellington.'

'I can come back tomorrow.'

'No. Please, Pagan,' Janet said persuasively, 'I think you need to see a doctor.'

'I feel fine.'

'Do you?' Janet gave Pagan a serious look. 'Not having any headaches?'

Pagan looked away quickly. 'Not really.' She rose from the chair with less than her usual grace. 'Look, I can't stay. I've got an appointment with my clairvoyant today. Do you have any idea how long you have to wait for a sitting with Iris?'

'No,' Janet said firmly. 'But I've got a very good idea what happens when you ignore the symptoms of pre-eclamptic toxaemia.'

Pagan's eyes widened.

'It could be serious, Pagan,' Janet continued quietly. 'Sit down until I can get Dr Spencer to look at you.'

Pagan sat, looking mutinous. Janet went into the office.

'Is Oliver back yet, Sandy?'

Sandy shook her head. Janet looked at her watch. Nearly 3.30 p.m. The boys should be arriving any minute, now. Hopefully she could keep them well away from Jamie. She smoothed down her hair distractedly. 'I'll have to think of some way to keep

Pagan happy until he gets back,' she told Sandy. 'I can't let her go without seeing Oliver.'

'Why?' The query came from Jamie who entered the office carrying a patient file.

'She's got fluid retention, proteinuria and raised blood pressure. She's thirty-eight weeks pregnant.'

'What's the BP?' Jamie put down the file.

'One-thirty over ninety.'

'Could be pre-eclampsia,' Jamie announced. 'I'll have a look at her.'

'No!' Janet said sharply.

'I beg your pardon?' Jamie's tone was amazed. 'Is there a problem with me seeing this patient?'

'Yes—there is.'

Jamie's eyebrows rose. His gaze raked Janet, demanding an explanation.

'It's a complicated case,' Janet hedged. 'Pagan's not keen on doctors or medical intervention. She needs careful handling.'

'Which I'm not capable of?'

'I didn't say that.' Janet was aware of Sandy Smith's fascinated observation of them. 'You just don't know the patient.'

'And you don't trust me to deal with it.'

'I didn't say that either.' Janet was feeling flustered now.

'Oliver's back,' Sandy observed. 'I just saw his car go past the window.'

Jamie reached for a new file from his in-basket. 'In that case, I'll see Mrs Gordon,' he said smoothly. His angry glance at Janet jarred with his tone. 'Unless you have another objection, Janet?'

'Of course not.' Janet's smile was relieved as she watched him leave. Mrs Gordon was notoriously difficult to deal with. She might well be able to escape with her sons before Jamie emerged from his latest consultation. She caught Oliver and explained her concerns, turning to Sandy before following the doctor into the treatment room.

'The twins are walking here after school,' she warned her. 'Let me know as soon as they arrive, will you, please? I don't want them causing any problems.'

Oliver was taking Pagan's blood pressure again. 'I'm going to have a chat to your obstetrician,' he told his patient, 'but I suspect he'll want to admit you again for observation.'

'Ring him tomorrow,' Pagan pleaded. 'I haven't seen Iris for months. She'll be able to tell if there's a real problem.'

'This could be serious, Pagan,' Oliver warned. 'Sophie would say the same thing.'

'But I feel fine. I'm just a bit puffy and get the odd headache. I've only got a few days to go. I can put up with it.'

'This could get worse,' Oliver said, 'in which case it could threaten both you and the baby. You need bed rest and monitoring. If your blood pressure goes up any further it could mean that a Caesarean will be advised, especially as you're so close to full term.'

'You mean it might go away if I rest?'

Oliver nodded. 'But you need to rest in hospital so they can watch your blood pressure and kidney function carefully. I'm going to ring your consultant now.

Have a rest on the bed for the moment. You don't have any more patients coming in, do you, Janet?'

'No.' Janet glanced at the clock. Three forty-five p.m. The boys should be here. She was supposed to be tidying up, ready for a 4 p.m. departure.

Oliver returned within minutes. 'You're to go home, collect a bag and go straight to the hospital,' he told Pagan. 'They'll be expecting you. Will you do that?'

Pagan nodded reluctantly. 'I suppose I'll have to.'

Oliver looked at her sternly. 'I'll ring the hospital in half an hour. If you're not there I might just come looking for you.'

Pagan laughed. 'You wouldn't!'

'No. But Sophie would and she's due at the airport in a couple of hours.'

Janet left Pagan talking to Oliver. She hurried into the front office. 'Have the boys shown up yet?' she asked Sandy. She was too worried to let Jamie's presence in the office distract her. 'They should have been here half an hour ago.'

Jamie stared. Sandy shook her head apologetically, before turning away to deal with Mrs Gordon's account. Jamie was still staring.

'Do you mean to say you don't know where your children are?'

'Of course I do,' Janet snapped.

'Where?'

'Somewhere between here and school.' Janet tried to brush past Jamie. 'I'm going to go and look for them right now.'

Jamie caught her arm. The grip felt different to

yesterday's touch. He was trying to slow her down, not interrogate her.

'Do you want some help?'

'No, thanks.'

The grip tightened. Jamie lowered his voice. 'Why is that, Janet? Is it none of my business or is it just that you don't trust me?'

Oliver and Pagan moved through the archway. They were laughing loudly enough to cover Janet's angry whisper. 'Let go of me, Jamie.'

He let go, but followed Janet into the treatment room as she grabbed her bag and fished out her car keys. He pushed the door shut behind him.

'Nothing changes, does it, Janet?' He glanced at the closed door. 'I don't care that you don't trust me on a personal level. When you let it interfere with the job I'm here to do, it's a different matter. I can't work with someone who's going to make a public issue out of a lack of trust.'

'I didn't,' Janet denied vehemently. 'And I don't have time to try and explain right now.'

'You don't need to explain. It's simple. You don't trust me.' Jamie took a step closer. '*Do* you, Janet?'

Janet tossed her curls with an angry shake of her head. 'No, I don't.'

'You never did.'

'Oh, yes, I did,' Janet hissed. 'I trusted you far too much.'

'Huh!' The sound was scornful. 'Not for long.'

'Until I had good reason not to,' Janet fired back.

'Good reason! Someone else's lies, you mean.'

'And the rest.' Janet was giving as good as she was

getting as far as furious looks went. 'The evidence was, as they say, irrefutable.'

'What *evidence*?' Jamie made the word sound like a non-existent commodity. 'What *did* you use for the final conviction, Janet? Before you dumped me?'

'*Me?* Dumped *you*?' Janet's jaw sagged from the weight of her incredulity.

'Tell me, Janet,' Jamie demanded harshly. 'I'm very interested.'

'No.' Janet stepped around Jamie. 'I don't want to talk about it. It's ancient history and there's no point in dredging any of it up.'

'There's every point when it means you decide which patients I'm allowed to see. I'm not going to work in an atmosphere of mistrust.'

'Fine.' Janet had her back to him now. She didn't bother turning. 'Go somewhere else, then.'

The door opened in the short silence that followed Janet's angry suggestion. Sandy was smiling. 'The boys are sitting out in your car, Janet. They said they've been there all the time because they didn't want to get into any trouble.'

'Oh, thank goodness.' Janet's relief expressed itself in a huge grin at Sandy. 'I must have forgotten to lock the car. I'd better take them home.'

'Good idea.' The sarcastic comment behind her was hard to ignore. 'Looks like I'm not the only one who can't be trusted.'

The words still grated on Janet late that night. She sat at the kitchen table, nursing a mug of strong tea and brooding over the argument. The nerve of the man, saying *she* had dumped *him*! Jamie made it sound as though he really believed he'd been done an injustice. He *had* always protested his innocence but the evidence *had* been irrefutable. Not just what she'd seen with her own eyes. There had been the letter as well. The letter from Sharlene.

Janet shook her head. That was the second time she'd thought of her old room-mate in as many days. After so many years of burying any unpleasant recollections.

When had Sharlene started poisoning the potential relationship Janet and Jamie had had going? In expressing her envy over the prize Janet had landed? Moving in on Jamie, however willingly or otherwise the move had been received? Had it been in the form of that letter? Janet tried to remember. The name of her room-mate had even appeared in the conversation Janet and Jamie had had on their drive back to Glasgow after that magic day—and night—on the island of Iona. The conversation had been a memorable one.

It had only been when they'd reached the outskirts of the city on their return journey that the potential repercussions of their stay on Iona had been discussed.

'I should have thought of it,' Jamie had accused himself ruefully. 'I was just in such a hurry to get away.' His brown eyes had cast an anxious glance at his companion. 'I don't do this sort of thing very often.'

'I'm pleased to hear it,' Janet had responded primly. 'But I'm just as much to blame. Sharlene's told me often enough to carry something in my pocket.'

'Sharlene?'

'My room-mate. She's a lot more experienced than me in that department.' Janet had giggled. 'She probably hands out condoms along with coffee. Haven't you met her? She's working up in Theatre at the moment. Black hair—great figure.'

'I've seen her around.' Jamie had sounded offhand. He'd still looked worried. 'Do you think there's any chance you might be pregnant, Jan? What stage of your cycle are you?'

'I'm not sure,' Janet had admitted. 'Early, I think. I guess we'll just have to wait and see.'

'Don't worry.' Jamie had felt for her hand and had squeezed it tightly. 'I'm not about to run out on you, whatever happens.'

And he didn't. Two weeks later he dragged Janet out for drink as soon as she finished her late shift.

'I've got a registrar position in London,' he told her excitedly. 'It's a really fantastic opportunity. Will you come with me, Janna? Come and live with me in London?'

'Of course I will.' Janet had to shout above the noise of the crowded pub, making the most of the few minutes left until closing time.

Jamie shouted, too. 'I love you, Janet Muir.'

'I love you, too, Jamie McFadden.'

The noise from those close enough to overhear increased as they cheered. Jamie fought his way to the bar, his arm holding Janet firmly glued to his side, to persuade the barman to let them have another drink by way of celebration.

'We're closing,' he was told.

'We'll be quick,' Jamie promised.

They only managed half the drinks before they were told to leave. Despite the rain, they walked slowly, reluctant to reach a destination where they'd have to part.

'Where shall we live in London?' Janet asked.

'I don't care.' Jamie grinned. 'As long as I'm with you. You choose.'

'Be serious,' Janet scolded. 'London's expensive.'

Jamie did become serious. 'I know. And we'll have to find our own flat if we want to live together. It'll mean we'll both have to work if we're going to be able to afford it.' For a moment, Jamie's expression was grim. 'Let's keep our fingers crossed that you're not pregnant, Jan.'

Janet confided her fears to her room-mate, Sharlene.

'Good for you,' Sharlene congratulated her. 'I would have done the same thing myself. Lucky you, getting someone that gorgeous to fall for the baby trap. And a *doctor*, too! It'll be wedding bells, next.'

'I didn't *plan* it!' Janet said angrily. 'How could you even think such a thing, Sharlene?'

Sharlene merely shrugged and for the first time Janet wondered just how much they really had in common. As room-mates went, Sharlene had been great up till now—considerate, generous and light hearted. She'd taken Janet under her wing when she'd come to the Western, making life easier for the nervous new arrival. Faced with Janet's stunned disapproval, Sharlene tried to make amends.

'I know how hard it is to get some privacy around here. Why don't you get Jamie to come tomorrow, after you've finished your shift? I'll make myself scarce and I'm on night duty so I'll be away until 7 a.m. Jamie can sneak out early by the fire escape.'

'He wouldn't want to do something like that,' Janet protested.

'Ask him,' Sharlene advised. 'You might be surprised what they're prepared to do for what they want.'

So Janet had asked him and she had been surprised.

'I'll be waiting for you,' Jamie said. 'Leave the door unlocked.' He quirked an eyebrow suggestively. 'I should warn you—I can't resist a woman in uniform.'

Janet couldn't wait for her late duty to finish that evening. She'd noted the stomach cramps she had with pleasure. She even welcomed the inconvenient spotting which heralded the start of her period. It was a huge relief. Jamie didn't need to feel pressured into offering marriage. There was no obstacle to her finding a job in London to help with the rent on a flat. Janet rushed through her final duties and was rewarded with getting away ten minutes early.

Ten minutes extra with Jamie! Janet ran through the quiet hospital corridors and up the road to the nurses' quarters. She took the steps to her floor two at a time and flung open the door of her room with joyous anticipation. Jamie would be there, waiting for her...and Sharlene would be away all night.

Jamie *was* there. But so was Sharlene. Sharlene wasn't ready for work. She wasn't wearing her uniform. She wasn't wearing anything much at all, having not bothered with any underwear beneath her flesh-coloured, see-through slip. Worse than that, she was standing with her body pressed against Jamie's, her fingers locked in the waves of his blond hair and her lips firmly covering his. Jamie had his hands up in the air, as though caught in the act of surrender. Or maybe he was trying to escape detection, having heard Janet's rapidly approaching footsteps on the linoleum covered corridor.

Janet was stunned speechless. Jamie looked acutely embarrassed. Only Sharlene appeared able to handle the situation with any ease,

'Time I got to work,' she announced calmly. She hooked her uniform off the foot of her bed, slipping it over her head in a fluid movement. She stepped into her white shoes and collected her red cape from the back of the door. 'He's all yours,' she said in a stage whisper to Janet. 'For now.'

It was Jamie who broke the unbearably tense silence. 'Does your room-mate always jump on unsuspecting men like that?'

'Not that *I've* noticed,' Janet replied coldly. 'Not uninvited, anyway.'

'*I* didn't invite her.' Jamie ran his fingers through his hair and then wiped his mouth with the back of his hand. 'I got here a bit early, that's all. I can't stay, Janet. Brian's off sick and I've got to cover him for the night.'

Janet eyed him steadily. He looked very ill at ease

for someone telling the truth. She didn't *want* him to stay. Not now. Not until she knew what had really been going on. 'Why did you come, then, Jamie?'

'I didn't want you waiting for me, and it wasn't a message I could leave with whoever answers the phone in this place. And...I wondered whether you knew yet...about...you know?'

'Yes.' Janet was watching him closely. Was the tension because he was dreading the prospect of unplanned fatherhood? Or because he was dreading having to face an inquisition about his dalliance with Sharlene? He couldn't resist a woman in uniform, he'd said. Had Sharlene been wearing hers when he'd arrived? Janet looked away. 'I'm not pregnant, Jamie. My period started today.'

'Thank God!' Jamie's face lit up with relief. 'I was so worried. It's only a week until I have to leave for London. I've heard of room in a flat that's available close to the hospital but it would have been impossible with a baby. We'll need to share the place with Paul. He's a surgeon who used to work here.' His pager sounded as he swept Janet into his arms. 'Now there's nothing stopping us.' He kissed Janet swiftly before he left. 'Sleep well, love.'

But Janet didn't sleep at all. She was ready to head back to the wards when Sharlene returned in the morning.

'What the hell was that all about last night, Sharlene?' Janet demanded. 'What are you trying to do?'

'Nothing that hasn't been done before,' Sharlene told her impatiently. 'Or will be again. Grow up,

Janet. Did you really think someone like Jamie McFadden would be content with only one girlfriend? Pretending to be pregnant won't work, you know. Not with him.'

'I'm not,' Janet said quietly. 'I wasn't pretending and I'm not pregnant. And I don't believe that you mean anything to Jamie.'

'Ask him, then,' Sharlene suggested airily. 'Ask him how I know about that little birthmark just beside his left nipple.'

Janet gasped. She knew that birthmark very well. She'd felt its slightly different texture with her fingers...and her tongue.

'He'll deny it, of course,' Sharlene sneered. 'They all do. But can you really trust him?'

Jamie did deny it. He denied it vehemently. He was astonished and then angry that Janet could even suggest he had any kind of relationship going with *any-body* else.

'You don't trust me,' he accused Janet.

'I *saw* you kissing her.'

'You saw *her* kissing me.'

'She says it wasn't the first time and it won't be the last. She knows things—about you—that she could only know if you and she—'

'For God's sake!' Jamie was furious. 'I don't *be-lieve* this! I had no idea you were so jealous and suspicious.'

'And I had no idea that one woman wasn't enough for you.'

'I'm beginning to think that one woman is too many,' Jamie snapped. 'If you can't trust me, then we've got nothing.' He stared at Janet with a bitter expression. 'Thank God you're *not* pregnant. It could never have worked.'

With that, Jamie stormed out. He left for London at the end of the week without contacting her. Janet was devastated. She missed Jamie terribly and she could have done without the unwanted sympathy of her room-mate.

'They're all the same,' Sharlene informed Janet. 'But never mind. There are plenty more fish in the sea and maybe next time you'll *really* get pregnant.'

The atmosphere between the two women deteriorated rapidly over the next few weeks. Janet requested a room change but Sharlene told her not to bother. She was leaving. Moving on. She moved out hurriedly, leaving half her possessions behind, at the time when Janet's next period began. It was much lighter than usual. Light enough to make Janet begin to wonder about the other symptoms she'd dismissed as being part of a stressful situation. Like the tiredness and faint nausea when faced with meals. It was another two weeks before Janet did anything about it, only to discover that she was, in fact, twelve weeks pregnant.

It took another week to agonise her way to the decision to tell Jamie. Apparently it wasn't that uncommon to have bleeding at the times you might have expected the first period or two after conception. It was more unusual for the bleeding to be heavy enough to seem normal, but the gynaecologist assured Janet that it didn't necessarily mean she would have further problems with the pregnancy. He then went on to drop the extra bombshell the scan had revealed. She was expecting twins.

It had been seven weeks since Jamie had left without a word. Three weeks since Sharlene had also left. Any connection hadn't occurred to Janet. When she persuaded the girl in Administration to give her Jamie's forwarding address and telephone number in London, the last thing she expected to hear on making the call was the voice of her former room-mate.

'Sharlene?' Janet's voice was an incredulous squeak. 'What are *you* doing there?'

'Living here—what do you think?' Sharlene laughed. 'I thought I'd just turn up and see what happened.' Sharlene lowered her voice confidentially. 'And you know what, Janet? I think the baby trap might work this time.'

'You mean you're…you're…?' Janet couldn't bring herself to say the word.

Sharlene had no such difficulty. 'Pregnant? You bet. Do you want an invitation to the wedding?'

'Oh… No, thanks, Sharlene.' Janet's desperate gaze fell on the pile of mail waiting for the nurses' home residents to collect from the front table. A letter addressed to herself lay on the top. Her older sister, Liz, had been a dreadful correspondent ever since her marriage had foundered and she had left two years ago on a working holiday in Australia and New Zealand. Janet's paralysed brain finally began functioning again as she registered the postmark on the letter. 'Actually,' she told Sharlene a little faintly, 'I'm thinking of going away. I might go and visit my sister in New Zealand.'

'Good idea!' Sharlene sounded very enthusiastic. 'Anyway, I suppose you really rang to talk to Jamie, seeing as you didn't know I was here. He's in the bath but I'll go and drag him out if you like.'

'No, don't bother.' The thought of Sharlene in the same room as a naked James McFadden made Janet feel sick. 'It was nothing important. 'Bye, Sharlene.'

The letter from Sharlene arrived a few days later. She wanted the rest of her possessions sent on. It was important, she said, to get properly settled now that a baby was on the way. They would need to move after the wedding because the flat would be too crowded and she didn't fancy hauling a pram up the stairs. Sharlene hoped Janet would enjoy the southern hemisphere.

The notion born of desperation took firmer root very quickly. Janet was four months pregnant when she left Scotland to join her sister. Liz was eight years older than Janet. She was also a nurse and had taken over the role of a parent when their mother had died ten years ago. She was only too happy to take her younger sister under her wing again, supporting her through her pregnancy and the early delivery of her two tiny sons. Liz continued to support Janet until the twins were nearly two, until Janet persuaded the immigration authorities to let her stay in the country permanently to raise her New Zealand-born children and grant her New Zealand citizenship. Until she landed a job as a practice nurse in a thriving general practice clinic. Then her older sister's itchy feet got the better of her. Liz left to take a position as a nurse on a cruise liner, confident that Janet was now content and capable of coping with her new life.

Janet *had* been content. She had been coping extremely well. Right up until two days ago when Jamie McFadden had reappeared. How could he even remotely expect her to trust him? And how dared he act as though he'd been the injured party? No wonder Janet didn't trust men any more. Not on a personal level.

Not on *any* level as far as James McFadden was concerned.

CHAPTER FIVE

'GOOD morning, Janet.'

'Good morning, Jamie.' Janet gave him only a brief glance before returning her gaze to the new batch of test results in front of her. Maybe he would take the hint from her deliberate coolness that she didn't want his company right now. In fact, she could do without it altogether. But Jamie seemed oblivious. So much for the old telepathy. He stood beside her—close beside her—and began reading the result forms over her shoulder.

'Who's Gareth Kelly?' he asked with interest.

'One of Josh's patients.' Janet moved her arm so that it wasn't in contact with the leather jacket Jamie had yet to discard for the morning. 'He had a raised cholesterol level and his blood pressure's been a bit high recently so Josh sent him in for these glucose tolerance tests. He's at risk for diabetes.'

'So I see.' Jamie leaned closer, reading the figures. 'What was his cholesterol level like?'

Janet picked up the sheaf of results still awaiting filing from last week and flipped through them. 'Total cholesterol was 6.5. HDL was 0.8. Ratio of 8 to 1.'

'Hmm. The HDL needs to come up a bit. What's his weight like?'

'Too high.'

'Does he smoke?'

'No.'

'Any family history of heart disease?'

'His father died at sixty-five with a heart attack.'

'What average is his blood pressure running at?'

'One-eighty over one-oh-five.'

Jamie was staring at Janet. 'How do you know all that? You're not even looking at his file.'

Janet shrugged. 'I've seen him a few times. Maybe I have a good memory.' She gave Jamie a pointed look. Her memory was excellent and wasn't confined to patient details.

Jamie's gaze was admiring. 'I'm impressed.'

'Do you want me to make an appointment for you to see Mr Kelly? I'll have to ring him this morning to let him know the results of this test.'

'Is he on any medication at present?'

'No. He's not keen on starting a drug regime. He thinks he might be able to cure himself with a good diet and some exercise.'

Jamie looked thoughtful. 'His blood pressure needs treating. I wouldn't want to start him with a diuretic in case the medication tipped him into having full diabetes. I think I'd put him on a beta blocker and possibly add in an ACE inhibitor. He might need some lipid-lowering agents as well if a change in diet isn't effective on the cholesterol level.'

Janet nodded. 'So you'd like to talk to him?'

'Yes. Make an appointment, please, Janet.' Jamie smiled at her. 'I've got a Mrs Harvey to see first this morning. What clues would your fantastic memory provide about her?'

'She's in her eighties, is on a beta blocker for hypertension and takes aspirin because she had a heart attack about nine years ago. She has trouble with her feet—probably gout.'

Jamie was back at the door of the treatment room ten minutes later. He winked at Janet. 'Could you take a blood test to measure Mrs Harvey's serum uric acid levels, please?'

'Certainly.' Janet tried to keep her tone coolly professional but it was hard not to feel satisfied that her guess had been correct. 'Come in, Mrs Harvey. This won't take long.'

Janet saw two more patients, before taking a break for a cup of tea at 10.30 a.m. Oliver was in the staffroom. So was Jamie.

'At least it's not too busy just now,' Oliver was saying as Janet entered. 'I'm sorry to land the extra patients on you, Jamie. Maybe Sophie will be well enough to come in this afternoon. She's planning a quick visit to the hospital to check on Mr Collins and our pregnant gypsy, Pagan Ellis.'

'I'll cope.' Janet saw the gratitude in Oliver's expression as Jamie smiled at him.

'You're a champion, mate.' Oliver grinned. 'Maybe you'd like to consider staying on. At the rate we're going, Sophie's going to need some rather extended maternity leave.'

Janet almost groaned aloud. She stared at Jamie, feeling like a rabbit caught in an oncoming car's headlights. He smiled back at her innocently.

'I'll certainly give the idea some consideration,' he said cheerfully. 'I wouldn't want to outstay my welcome, though.'

Janet tore her gaze away. What welcome? she thought dourly. Poking a teabag into her mug, she drowned it with boiling water. She barely heard Oliver excuse himself as she added milk and sugar to her drink. It was only when she went to sit down that Janet realised she was alone with Jamie. She stopped short and picked up her mug again, her eyes on the door as she planned her retreat to the treatment room.

'Sit down, Janet,' Jamie invited.

'I'm a bit busy, actually.'

'No, you're not. It's nice and quiet out there.' Jamie was watching her closely. 'Sit down. I think I owe you a bit of an apology.'

Janet was startled into compliance. She sat.

'I was angry when I thought you didn't trust me to deal with your pregnant patient, but Oliver has explained her history and I can see why you were concerned.' Jamie smiled a little sheepishly. 'I must admit I was also a bit thrown to discover you had children. Somehow I just hadn't expected it. I don't know why. You're quite right—it's none of my business. We said we'd forgive and forget.'

'*You* said that, not me,' Janet said quietly.

'Let's start again, shall we?' Jamie suggested. 'As in, fancy meeting you here, Janet. What's been happening since I last saw you?' Jamie smiled winningly. 'I *am* interested, you know.'

'Why?' Janet asked desperately. 'Why do you want to know? Why did you come here, Jamie? Did you know *I* was here?'

'Not precisely. I knew you'd come to New Zealand

to visit your sister. Your friend told me. What was her name? Sharon? Shelley?'

'Sharlene,' Janet muttered.

'That's right. Sharlene. How could I forget?'

'How could you indeed?' Janet flashed Jamie a bitter glance but Jamie merely shrugged.

'Water under the bridge now. Anyway, London was just what I needed at the time. A big hospital, lots of hard work and all the distractions a big city could provide.'

Janet snorted. What had *he* needed distraction from?

Jamie nodded at her disparaging sound. 'That's exactly how I felt after a couple of years. I decided that maybe I didn't want to specialise after all. I wanted to get out of hospital life and into a community. Maybe something small and rural with a few wind-swept hills and a sea view.' Jamie paused. 'I often used to remember Iona and how peaceful it was,' he said softly. 'Did you?'

Janet took a large gulp of scalding tea. She did *not* want to discuss the island of Iona.

Jamie shrugged. 'I ended up in a rural practice in the Midlands which wasn't quite what I'd had in mind. Then I went back to Glasgow. I got a job in a practice in Hillhead, just a wee way from the Western Infirmary.'

'Did you?' Janet tried to sound politely interested. Her voice had enough of an edge to let Jamie know she had no desire to discuss that particular area either. She took a more cautious sip of her drink.

'I started going to that pub on the corner of Byres Road. Remember it?'

'Not really.' Janet's heart was hammering. The pub where they had shouted their love for each other. Where they'd only had half a drink to celebrate the start of their planned future together.

'Oh.' Jamie sounded disappointed. 'Anyway, I met an O and G registrar from the Western there quite often. He came from New Zealand and told me a lot about the country. I started to get interested. He came from Christchurch and he made the South Island sound far more attractive than up north. Larger and less populated, with vast areas of unspoilt natural beauty. Made me think it would be like Iona—on a grand scale.'

'So you decided to emigrate? Just like that?'

'Not at all. I spent a long time thinking about it. Not emigrating—just a working holiday.' Jamie beamed at Janet. 'And here I am. OK, your turn.'

Janet ignored the invitation. 'So you didn't know I was here?'

'How could I? I haven't seen any of your friends for years.'

Janet twisted a curl of her hair in her fingers. She kept her eyes on the table. 'Would you have come— if you *had* known?'

Jamie was silent long enough for Janet to look up. His brown eyes held her gaze. 'Yes,' he said quietly. 'I think perhaps I would have.'

Janet swallowed painfully. There was no sinister motive for Jamie's arrival here. He had accepted that her children had been fathered by someone else. Did that mean he genuinely still found something attractive about her? Did she *want* him to?

'I'd better get on,' she said hurriedly. 'We've probably got a whole bunch of patients waiting by now.'

Janet could feel Jamie's gaze following her as she rinsed out her mug and left the room. The conversation with Jamie had raised more questions than it had answered. Why was Sharlene water under the bridge and had Jamie really been unable to remember her name? Why had Jamie been obsessed with images of Iona? Above all, why would he still have wanted to come if he'd known she was here? Even framing the question, it gave Janet a peculiar sensation that could almost be excitement. Fortunately, she had no time to ponder. Someone needing attention was waiting in the treatment room.

Mary Todd was a young woman who lived next door to St David's. Janet spoke to her for only a minute, before ducking out to the main office. Jamie was in there. He was picking up the file for his next patient, Taylor Langdon, a young Down's syndrome girl. Janet touched his arm.

'Have you got a minute, Jamie?'

'Of course.' Jamie glanced at her keenly. 'Is there a problem?'

'I've got Mary Todd in the treatment room. She lives next door and she was stung by a bee about ten minutes ago. She's feeling a bit odd. Could you have a look at her, please?'

'Does she have a known allergy?'

'No.' Janet was ahead of Jamie, moving fast. 'But

she's itchy all over now and says her breathing feels a bit tight.'

'Hello, Mary. I'm Dr McFadden.' Jamie moved with deceptive calm as he unhooked his stethoscope from around his neck. 'You had a wee argument with a bee, I understand.'

Mary nodded. 'I feel sick, Dr McFadden. I've got terrible cramps in my stomach.'

Jamie had lifted the back of the woman's T-shirt to position the stethoscope. He glanced at Janet who was lifting a cardboard vomit container from her cupboard. 'Draw up .5 milligrams of adrenaline, would you, Janet? Intramuscular.'

Janet's hands were shaking slightly as she cracked the ampoule of adrenaline and slotted a needle into its neck. If Mary was having an anaphylactic reaction to the bee venom, then this could be a serious emergency. Jamie took the syringe from the kidney dish and then raised an eyebrow questioningly.

'Och, sorry.' Janet whirled around to pick up the empty ampoule from the bench so Jamie could check that the medication was the correct one. Had she checked the expiry date? Janet felt a cold prickle of perspiration break out on her back. Of course she had. Why did she feel such an unusual lack of confidence?

'Let's have some oxygen, Janet,' Jamie suggested, as he injected the adrenaline into Mary's arm. His hand ran down the woman's arm and Janet could see that urticarial lumps had formed. Another sign of a severe allergic reaction.

Janet picked up the cardboard container as Mary retched but Jamie plucked it from her hand. 'The oxygen,' he reminded her. 'High flow. Have you got a nebuliser mask?'

'Yes, of course.' Janet could hear the wheeze Mary was producing between the coughs which had replaced the retching. She fumbled to open the plastic bag containing the mask. Jamie took the packaging from her.

'You're doing fine,' he said quietly. 'Dilute 2 milligrams of adrenaline with 4 mililitres of saline for the mask and then draw up another intramuscular dose.'

This time Jamie only gave the ampoule a cursory glance before adding the medication to the attachment on the mask. Mary was still sitting up on the bed, leaning forward. Her breathing sounded even more laboured. She looked up at Janet.

'I'm going to die,' she said desperately. 'I can't breathe!'

Jamie touched the swelling Janet could see around Mary's eyes. 'You're going to be fine, Mary. Just concentrate on your breathing.' Jamie still appeared perfectly calm. 'Try and get a blood pressure for me, Janet. Where do you keep your angiocaths?'

'I'll get one.' Janet pulled open a drawer. 'What gauge do you want?'

'Wide bore. A fourteen if you have one.'

Janet handed him the IV cannula, a tourniquet and antiseptic wipes. Then she wrapped the blood-pressure cuff around Mary's other arm.

'One-oh-five over sixty-five,' she reported.

Jamie had the needle poised over Mary's vein. He

nodded briefly. 'You'll feel a bit of a stab here, Mary. Hang on. You're doing really well.'

Janet was impressed by the skill Jamie demonstrated in inserting the wide bore IV line. She had a saline flush ready in a syringe as Jamie attached the plug to the line. Then she uncurled the tubing of the IV giving set, inserting the sharp point into the port on the bag of fluid. Mary was sounding worse, despite the medication, and Janet bit her lip as Jamie helped Mary lie flat on the bed, her level of consciousness clearly dropping.

'Get Oliver, would you, please, Janet?'

Oliver abandoned his patient instantly. Janet paused only briefly by the front office. 'Call an ambulance, please, Sandy.'

Sandy's face paled. 'Not *again*!'

'Tell them we have a severe anaphylactic reaction,' Janet instructed. 'It's urgent.' She shut the door of the treatment room behind her. Sandy would have to cope. She herself was needed in here.

'I've just given her some IV adrenaline.' Jamie had his hand on Mary's wrist. 'She's throwing off a few ectopic beats.'

'Hook up the life-pack monitor, Janet,' Oliver instructed. He turned back to Jamie. 'I think we'd better intubate her. Are you happy to do that?'

Jamie nodded. He caught Janet's eye as she unwrapped the sterile pack containing the equipment needed. The glance seemed to convey the message that Oliver, at least, trusted Jamie. It also conveyed a question. Did she?

'What size tube do you want, Jamie?' Janet queried briskly. 'A 7.5?'

'Thanks.' Jamie picked up the laryngoscope and fitted on the blade. He reached for the tube Janet was holding only seconds later. His brief smile was appreciative. Of what? Janet wondered. Her ability to assist in an emergency? Or the fact that she obviously trusted his professional skill?

The trust had been well placed. By the time the paramedics arrived Mary's condition was stable enough to transfer her to hospital. Oliver went with her, leaving Jamie to cope with the queue that Sandy had accumulated.

Janet moved into high gear. She knew most of these patients and could fill Jamie in on their histories more quickly than reading their notes could have done. She could see them first, taking blood pressures, ECGs and eliciting details of problems which could then be relayed concisely to Jamie for investigation. They started with young Taylor Langdon who needed any illness monitored carefully because of her congenital heart problems. Between them, they saw twelve patients by the time Oliver returned an hour and a half later. He had Sophie with him.

'Look who I found at the hospital.' He smiled. 'I thought we might be in dire need of her assistance.'

'And the waiting room's empty,' Sophie said accusingly. 'What did you do? Put up a "Closed" sign?'

'Janet and I worked like a well oiled machine,' Jamie told them. 'There's nothing we can't cope with, is there, Janet?'

'No.' Janet was still feeling exhilarated by the fast pace she'd been working at. Jamie was right. Things had gone incredibly smoothly and they *had* worked very well together. Something had clicked—professionally, at least. Of necessity, they'd established a rapport which had enabled them to trust each other's judgement. It was surprising how good it felt. Janet's grin was directed at Jamie before she turned it on her colleagues. 'You two can go and have a second honeymoon. We'll look after the shop.'

'That reminds me.' Sophie reached into her shoulder-bag. 'There's a postcard from Josh and Toni that arrived this morning. They're in Jamaica.'

'And missing all the fun,' Oliver said sadly. 'Two emergencies in the same week. Something's changed about this place and I'm not sure I can keep up with it.'

Janet moved away from the group. Something had certainly changed. After this morning she was almost inclined to think it might be for the better. If she and Jamie could actually extend their rapport, maybe they could achieve some kind of understanding—a resolution that might even provide an explanation, if not an apology. Maybe then Janet would be able to forgive Jamie and put the past firmly where it belonged. She might even be able to restore a little of her faith in her own judgement and move on without being haunted by such a momentous personal failure.

It wouldn't be easy, of course, but Janet was prepared to meet him part way if Jamie admitted his blame. To forget was impossible. To forgive?

Maybe.

The exhilaration stayed with Janet as she worked steadily through the afternoon. She wasn't dreading encounters with Jamie any more. The eye contact they had was more frequent and less tense. Janet even found herself smiling at Jamie when no one else was around to notice. For his part, Jamie seemed to be looking for reasons to come into the treatment room.

One reason was quite legitimate. He had a patient with a splinter buried deep in his heel. Janet provided the scalpel and tweezers needed to remove the foreign object, then she cleaned up the infected wound and dressed it. Jamie had no patient to bring with him when he returned a short time later.

'Thanks for your help,' he said. ''I hope that didn't disrupt your timetable too much.'

'Not at all. You timed it just right. I had a quiet spell.'

'You did a great job this morning. I wouldn't have managed without you.'

Janet looked away quickly, a spot of colour highlighting each cheek. 'It's just part of my job, Jamie. It's what a practice nurse does.' She pulled open the door of the autoclave. 'Och!' Janet blew on her fingers.

Jamie took a step closer. 'You should open that door a bit more slowly.'

'Thanks,' Janet muttered. 'I'll try and remember that.'

Jamie took hold of her hand. 'Let me see.'

'No.' Janet tried to pull her hand free. 'It's fine.'

Jamie didn't let go and Janet stopped tugging. Jamie turned her hand over, examining the reddened fingers. He took a deep breath as he bent his head. 'Do you *still* use that herbal shampoo?'

'I…I don't think so.' Janet tried to concentrate on her hand but Jamie's fingers were stroking it. And the sensations the contact provoked were more disturbing than the thought of him noticing the smell of her hair.

She could hear the change in Jamie's breathing and her own quickened in response. Was he feeling the same stirrings of desire? He seemed reluctant to drop her hand. Janet gave a little tug.

'It's fine,' she told him.

Jamie let go slowly. 'Yes,' he agreed. 'No damage done.'

Janet was caught by the intense gaze from those dark brown eyes. She cleared her throat nervously. 'Um…Jamie?'

'Mmm?'

'Maybe we could…should…um.'

'Should what, Janet?' If anything, the gaze became even more intense. Janet had the uncomfortable feeling that he knew the reason for her lack of coherence and was quite happy to encourage it.

Janet took a step back. She couldn't think straight, standing this close to Jamie. She cleared her throat. 'I thought maybe we should have a talk,' she said in a rush. 'Not here. Somewhere where we'd have a bit more space and time.'

'Sounds good to me,' Jamie said agreeably. 'We've still got a bit of catching up to do. On your side, anyway. Right now, though, I'd better go and catch up with some patients. I've got a 3.30 appointment with some children who won't stop coughing.'

Janet watched him leave as she emptied the auto-clave. The twins should be here any minute and they would have plenty of company in the waiting room. The numbers of children always increased after school hours and the noise level right now suggested that today's younger patients were rather high-spirited.

Suddenly struck by the horrible thought that it might be *her* children responsible for the gleeful shrieks of laughter, Janet dived for the door. She stood in the archway and watched in dismay as Jamie strode across the waiting room to deal with the badly behaved small boy who was swinging on the drape hanging on one side of the bay window.

'Cut that out,' Jamie ordered sternly. 'Leave the curtain alone this minute.' The small boy turned quickly in surprise, still hanging onto the base of the curtain. Another child was clearly behind the drape, still giggling as it clutched at the disappearing fabric. The curtain rail sagged and then snapped at the in-creasing burden. A small shrouded figure fell, landing on top of the culprit Jamie had just admonished.

Janet heard Sandy giggle as she watched the un-folding drama. The other mothers present were also watching, keeping their own children under strict su-pervision. Janet knew she should go in and sort out the chaos her children had created, but she couldn't move. It was too much, seeing Jamie about to meet his sons for the first time.

The shrouded child rolled around vigorously, trying to extricate itself. The heaving puddle of fabric on the floor suddenly parted as a small head emerged. Jamie frowned as he looked from one boy to the other. Then he nodded slowly and sighed.

'You're Janet Muir's twins, aren't you?'

The boys nodded eagerly. 'I'm Rory,' one said with a cheeky grin. 'And that's Adam.'

'You're not behaving very well, are you?' Jamie growled.

Rory's grin vanished abruptly. 'It was an accident.'

'Accidents don't happen when you behave yourselves. Sit there,' Jamie ordered firmly, pointing to the window-seat. 'Boys that are nearly six years old should be capable of sitting and waiting without causing trouble.'

'Oh, no!' Janet muttered under her breath. Her feet began to move. She knew it was too late but she had to try. 'Adam! Rory!' she exclaimed. 'What on earth is going on? What happened to that curtain?'

The twins had scrambled to comply with Jamie's order to sit on the window seat but they ignored their mother. Their small faces were mutinous.

'We're *not* nearly six,' Rory said indignantly. 'We were six on our last birthday.'

'Rory's right,' Adam added. 'We're going to be seven soon.'

Jamie said nothing. He looked away from the two small faces and turned, very deliberately, to face Janet.

'Is that right?' he murmured casually. His gaze speared Janet. 'You were quite right, Janet.' Jamie's voice was too low to be overheard by the other waiting patients. He aimed his words with icy precision.

'We *should* have a talk.'

CHAPTER SIX

THE rights and wrongs of the situation were painfully clear.

James McFadden had the right to know that he was the father of the twins. The twins had the right to know who their father was. Janet was in the wrong. She was entirely to blame and the arguments she'd effectively mustered in her defence over the years had gone out of the window the instant she'd seen the three of them standing together in the waiting room.

Jamie also had the right to be angry. It was all too easy to see the situation from his point of view. It didn't matter now many other relationships—or children—Jamie had had. The twins were his sons and he had been denied knowledge of their existence. He had missed nearly seven years of their lives.

Janet shivered. The fire had burned out long ago and she should have gone to bed then but what was the point? Her fear of the inevitable confrontation with Jamie made the prospect of sleep highly unlikely. What would he demand of her? And what was she prepared to give?

'Oh, God,' Janet groaned softly. What if he decided he wanted custody? It did happen in some cases when the mother was deemed unfit. Jamie had been at St David's for four days. In that time he'd heard about the boys incinerating Mrs Carpenter's shed, had seen their mother unaware of their exact whereabouts for a considerable period of time after school and had observed their unruly and destructive behaviour in the waiting room.

It would also be very easy for him to discover their learning difficulties at school and their relatively deprived living conditions at home. A damp, cold house that contributed to winter ills. A garden that was far too small for two boisterous boys to play in. Any solicitor could have a field day painting the dismal picture of the life Janet provided for the twins. Could she afford to defend herself?

She couldn't afford *not* to defend herself. There was no way Janet was going to give up any part of her sons. She would fight any attack James McFadden mounted, tooth and nail. The attack would come, there was no doubt about that. And Janet would be ready for it.

She was ready for it as soon as she stepped through the door of St David's on Friday morning. She had even anticipated the look of contempt she received from Jamie and she didn't flinch at the controlled fury she sensed beneath the stare. Janet straightened her back. Any time, her body posture suggested. She was ready.

The readiness wore off during the morning, however. How could patients come and go with their minor ailments and complaints, oblivious to the detonation waiting to happen? How could Oliver and Sophie cope with their patient load, thinking that all was finally running smoothly after a difficult week? And why was Jamie biding his time, calmly charming patients and staff? Even Outboard had taken to following him at every opportunity and it was Jamie's lap the cat chose when the staff gathered for a break at lunchtime.

Janet was a nervous wreck by then. She hoped no one would notice that her hands were trembling as she made herself a cup of tea. Intending to take the drink back to her room, Janet was dismayed by the level of concern Oliver's tone indicated.

'Come and sit down, Janet. You look like you've had a tough morning.'

'I've got a few things to get on with.' Janet tried to excuse herself. 'I'm leaving a bit earlier today.'

'Sit!' Oliver commanded. 'We don't have a single patient on the premises at the moment and anything else can wait.' He looked more closely at Janet. 'Are you not sleeping well at the moment?'

'I'm fine, thanks, Oliver.' Janet avoided looking at Jamie. She smiled at Sophie instead. 'More to the point, how are *you*, Sophie?'

'Awful,' Sophie admitted. 'I haven't thrown up today but I still feel like I'm going to all the time.'

'Nothing worse than nausea,' Jamie sympathised. 'Did you get morning sickness, Janet, when you were expecting the twins?'

Sophie looked from Jamie to Janet, her surprise at Jamie knowing about the twins evident. Janet tried to sound casual.

'Not really.'

'You were lucky,' Oliver observed. 'It can be even more of a problem with twins.'

'Everything's more of a problem with twins.' Janet

smiled, trying to lighten the suddenly charged atmosphere. She could feel Jamie's cool stare. Was he waiting for more evidence of her inadequate mothering skills? 'I mean, not a problem exactly. It's just more...noticeable.'

Sophie was watching Jamie. 'The twins are never a problem,' she declared. 'They're terrific kids.' She hesitated briefly. 'Have you met them, Jamie?'

'I had the pleasure yesterday,' Jamie said blandly.

Janet stood up hurriedly. 'That was one of the things I needed to do—arrange for someone to come and fix the curtain rail. I am sorry about that, Oliver.'

'It doesn't matter,' Oliver assured her. 'It's not as if we ever close those curtains. I think we'll just take the other one down as well and let some more light in.'

Sophie rose to follow Janet. 'I must go, too. I want to pay a quick visit to Mr Collins before he goes home from hospital today. I'd better drop in on Pagan and make sure she's behaving herself as well.'

'Hang on!' Oliver jumped to his feet. 'I want to get our first-aid kit out of the car. It's high time I updated it and I may as well take advantage of a quiet spell.'

Janet shut herself into the treatment room, knowing her respite would be brief. Sandy was having the afternoon off as a reward for having coped so well with her first week full time, and Janet would have to juggle reception duties with her own tasks. She would just wait a few minutes until Oliver came back inside and reduced the chance of an unchaperoned encounter with Jamie. Janet wasn't ready for the confrontation any more. She needed time. Preferably a lot of it.

A minute ticked past. Then another. Janet went to the side window of the treatment room and peered out. She could see down to the car park at the back of the old house. Oliver and Sophie were standing beside their car. The first-aid kit was open on the bonnet and the two doctors appeared to be scrutinising and discussing its contents. Janet watched anxiously, so intent on her desire to see Oliver head back inside that she didn't hear the door open and close quietly behind her.

'Am *I* the boys' father, Janet?'

Janet jumped at the voice behind her. She turned quickly, her face pale. After hesitating for a long moment, she nodded mutely.

'Do Adam and Rory *know* they have a father?'

'Yes, of course they do.'

'What have you told them?'

'That their father lives in Scotland. That we don't live together because...'

'Because what, Janet?' Jamie had his back against the door. His arms were folded and his face looked as though it had been carved from granite.

Janet's mouth went dry. She tried to swallow. Jamie's lip curled fractionally. 'Never mind. What I really want to know is why you lied to me.'

Janet found her voice. 'I *didn't*!'

'You told me you weren't pregnant.'

'I didn't think I was. I got my period on time. I even had another one.'

'Really.' The word was blatantly scornful. Janet felt the blood return to her face with a rush.

'It's *true*.'

Jamie took a deep breath and let it out again slowly. 'I don't believe you.'

'I can't help that. It's *still* the truth.'

'And I *still* don't believe you.' Jamie's gaze held Janet pinned. 'To think that you accused *me* of lying and decided that I was untrustworthy.' He snorted incredulously. 'And all the time it was you being dishonest and manipulative. Maybe you'd planned on solo parenthood all along and I was just a convenient stud.'

Janet could feel her anger gathering. Giving her strength. She *was* telling the truth. How dared Jamie not believe her?

'Did it not occur to you that I had the right to know?'

'Of course it did. I was going to tell you. I tried to ring you in London but you…you didn't answer the phone. Your…' Janet paused, trying to sort the jumble of angry thoughts into coherency. What had Sharlene been to him at that point? His flatmate? Lover? His fiancée?

'You're lying,' Oliver accused her quietly. 'Again.' He shook his head. 'You never had any intention of telling me. Any intention of communicating with me at all.'

'I *did*!' Janet insisted. She could hear the telephone ringing in the office.

'I suppose you're going to tell me you answered the letter as well.'

'What letter?'

Jamie's expression was disgusted. 'Don't try telling me you never received it. I *know* you got it. Sharlene told me she'd make sure you did.'

Janet gaped at him, dimly aware that the phone had stopped. Jamie *knew* about that letter? Perhaps even encouraged the writing of it? 'You mean…about the baby? About getting married?'

'Amongst other things.'

'Yes, I got the letter.' Janet's voice was stronger now. Her tone was clipped. 'The message was perfectly clear.'

'And did you answer it?'

'No.'

'Why not?'

Janet shook her head slowly. 'What more was there to say, Jamie? It was finished.'

'But it wasn't finished, was it, Janet?' The phone was ringing again. The sound grew suddenly more strident as Jamie wrenched the door open. 'It's still not finished,' he warned Janet. 'Not by a long shot.'

'What is that supposed to mean?' Janet demanded. She was ready to fight now. That he could accuse her of lying and almost in the same breath admit that her reasons for not trusting him had been justified was quite unbelievable. 'Just what do you intend trying to do, Jamie?'

'I haven't decided.' Jamie's tone was cold, his face set. 'I'll let you know when I have. In the meantime…' Jamie turned away '…why don't you answer that damned telephone?'

Janet did answer the damned telephone. She barely

registered listening to the caller's tale of woe and she made the appointment automatically. She felt furious. She'd been telling the truth and Jamie had no intention of believing her. Being falsely accused wasn't something that had happened to Janet since she'd been a child. It was so *unfair* and she had no means of proving her innocence. She hated Jamie McFadden. Just as much as he obviously hated her. What a mess!

Janet stared at the telephone as it began ringing again. A line of thought was trying to untangle itself and she wasn't sure she wanted it to. Jamie had been this angry at her once before. When she hadn't believed him. She'd known him quite well enough to recognise the anger as genuine. Now she was experiencing it herself and she knew why. It was because the accusation was unjustified. She was innocent. But that line of reasoning couldn't be applied in retrospect to Jamie. Or could it? Janet had been wrong in her decision not to let Jamie know about the twins. Was that the only thing she had been wrong about?

The phone was still ringing as Oliver breezed through the front door, carrying his first-aid kit. 'Aren't you going to answer that, Jan?'

Janet pushed her confusion firmly aside. She reached for the receiver. 'Good afternoon,' she said stiffly. 'St David's Medical Centre. Janet speaking.'

For a large man, Jamie made himself remarkably unobtrusive for the remainder of Friday afternoon. Janet was far too busy to allow personal problems to interfere with her duties. It was a relief to concentrate on work. Sophie returned by mid-afternoon, looking

much brighter. Janet made her a cup of tea. Oliver
and Jamie came into the staffroom as Sophie sat down
at the table.

'Pagan's fine,' she reported. 'She's sitting cross-
legged on her bed in the ward, meditating to keep her
blood pressure down. She says she only needs to keep
it up for a few more days until the star signs are
exactly right and then it doesn't matter even if she
has to have a Caesarean. They might induce her next
week if things stay stable.'

'How's Mr Collins?' Oliver queried.

'Going home. Says he feels better than he has for
years. He says he'll come in on Monday with a copy
of his discharge summary so you can have an in-depth
discussion about future monitoring.'

Oliver grinned. 'Hey, Jamie. Are you planning on
coming back on Monday?'

Jamie raised an eyebrow. 'Why wouldn't I be?'

Oliver chuckled. 'I thought this last week might
have put you off St David's somewhat.'

Jamie's smile was relaxed. Janet was already moving towards the door but she knew he was watching
her. She could feel the gaze like a touch between her
shoulder blades.

'I'm not put off that easily, Oliver. I have every
intention of sticking it out.'

'Good for you.' Oliver was smiling broadly. 'In
that case, let me tell you about your new patient for
Monday morning.'

'Oliver—you wouldn't!' Sophie giggled.

Janet cleared the door, moving more rapidly. She
could still hear Oliver's warm approbation.

'This man is a champion,' he declared. 'If anyone can win with our Mr Collins, it's our Dr McFadden.'

Our Dr McFadden. So he was one of them now. Janet gritted her teeth. And he was a winner. What would that make Janet? The loser?

The weekend passed too swiftly. Janet's time with her sons was precious. Even the minor irritations of sibling arguments, sabotage of her housekeeping efforts and occasional accidental destruction seemed unimportant. Monday morning arrived and the boys were unusually keen to go to school. Janet was less than keen to return to St David's. Jamie had had a whole weekend to plan his campaign. Would today be when he chose to inform her of his decisions?

Sophie didn't look well again and Oliver was clearly worried about his wife.

'I thought complete bed rest over the weekend would help, but it hasn't,' he told Janet. He pulled a file from his in-basket. 'If this keeps up much longer I might admit her to hospital for a few days. She's bordering on dehydration.'

'Has she seen a specialist about it?'

'No.' Oliver brightened a little. 'We thought it was too early to choose one but that's a good thought, Janet. I'll arrange something today.' He spotted the arrival of Mr Collins and beat a hasty retreat from the reception area.

Sandy was fascinated by Mr Collins's account of his 'near death' experience.

'I was up in that corner, lassie,' Mr Collins told her, pausing to indicate the portion of the ceiling beside the broken curtain rail. Janet noted that Mr Collins's vocal volume control appeared to have been adjusted. It was the first time she'd ever heard him talking so quietly. 'I could see them working on me,' he said softly in awe. 'Dragging me back from the brink.'

'*Really?*' Sandy's eyes were round. Her tone was as hushed as that of Mr Collins. 'Was that when you heard the music?'

A small queue had formed behind Mr Collins. Janet decided it was time to intervene. 'Perhaps I could take your blood pressure, Mr Collins, while you're waiting to see the doctor. You should really be sitting down.' Janet glanced at the manila folder her patient was holding. 'Is that your discharge summary?'

'It's a copy of everything that went into my medical records,' Mr Collins told her proudly, 'including a detailed account of my angioplasty procedure. I know Dr Spencer will want to see it.'

'Actually, it's Dr McFadden who will be seeing you this morning, Mr Collins. He's our locum.'

'A locum?' Mr Collins looked alarmed. 'But he won't know anything about my history!'

'He's an excellent doctor,' Janet said soothingly. 'In fact, it was Dr McFadden who helped us save your life when you arrested.'

'Is that right? Part of the resuscitation team, was he?'

'Aye.' Janet nodded as she wrapped the blood-pressure cuff around Mr Collins's upper arm. 'You gave him a dramatic start to his stay with us. I'm sure he's looking forward to seeing how you are today.'

Mr Collins looked unconvinced. He eyed the inflating cuff. 'Pump that up a bit further,' he advised Janet. 'You'll find the systolic pressure about 160.'

Janet squeezed the bulb a few more times. 'You must have been seen by a lot of doctors who didn't know you in the hospital. Sometimes it helps to have a fresh perspective.'

Mr Collins nodded thoughtfully. 'You could be right there, lassie. And I can fill him in. I know what I'm talking about.'

'You do indeed, Mr Collins.' Janet deflated the cuff. 'One-sixty over ninety.'

Mr Collins sighed with satisfaction. 'I'm thinking of getting my own sphygmomanometer,' he told Janet, 'so I can monitor my own blood pressure. What brand would you recommend?'

'Ask Dr McFadden.' Janet suppressed a mischievous smile as she unwrapped the cuff. 'I'm sure he knows much more about the technical specifications than I do.'

Mr Collins had been in Jamie's room for nearly forty-five minutes when Oliver knocked on Janet's door.

'Have we got any chlorpromazine?'

'I think so.' Janet stood up from her desk. She raised her eyebrows. It wasn't a drug they used very often. Chlorpromazine was an antipsychotic that was effective in providing control in a crisis situation. 'Mr Collins isn't having delusions, is he? Full symphony orchestras backing up Jamie?'

Oliver grinned. 'I've just had a call from the manager of the supermarket down the road. May Little is creating a bit of a problem. The manager didn't know whether to call the police or an ambulance and rang me for advice. I said we'd pop down and have a look.'

Janet had found the drug in her cupboard. She drew up the required dose into a syringe and capped it firmly, putting it into an envelope with some antiseptic wipes and the empty ampoule.

'We probably won't need it,' Oliver said. 'She might just need to talk to someone who knows her.'

Jamie was in the front office as Oliver and Janet came out of the treatment room. He looked somewhat dazed.

'That was an unusual experience,' he murmured. 'Your Mr Collins is quite a character.'

'It gets better.' Oliver grinned. 'We're just off to the supermarket to see another one.' His grin faded as he noticed Sophie. She had come out of the side room and was now leaning against the wall, her hand over her eyes.

'What's wrong, Sophie?'

'I don't feel good,' Sophie said unhappily. 'I think I might be going to faint.'

Oliver shoved the envelope he was holding towards Jamie. 'Go with Janet,' he instructed. 'I'll have to look after Sophie.'

Jamie looked inside the envelope as he climbed into the car beside Janet. 'Chlorpromazine? What's all this about?'

'May Little is one of our regular patients.' Janet changed gear and pulled out onto the road. 'She's rather odd and has exhibited paranoid tendencies. She appears to be having some sort of crisis in the local supermarket.' Janet had her indicator on already. 'It's just in here. We were the closest help available.'

The manager of the small supermarket was waiting by the door. 'I'm glad to see you,' he said fervently. 'I didn't know what to do.'

'What's happened exactly?' Jamie asked.

They were being led through the produce department at a rapid pace. 'The lady apparently decided the closed circuit camera was watching her. She became very upset and barricaded herself into a corner with trolleys. Unfortunately, she's blocking the checkouts and shrieks if anyone touches the trolleys.' The manager turned sharply into an aisle. A small crowd of people stood at the other end. 'Now she's building some kind of a structure with tinned produce. She threw a can of asparagus at me when I tried to talk to her.'

Jamie nodded. They could see the chaos ahead. May Little was wearing the same hat and thick woollen coat Janet had last seen her in. The clothing was even more inappropriate given the warmth of the summery day today. May was talking aloud to herself and frantically pulling cans from the shelves, piling them into the trolleys parked around her. Bystanders were watching incredulously.

'See if you can move everyone away,' Jamie told the manager. 'Being watched isn't going to help. And call an ambulance. Miss Little is going to need to be admitted to hospital when we get her calm enough to move.' Jamie stepped forward. 'Hello, May,' he called loudly. 'I'm Dr McFadden. Janet Muir is here, too. You know Janet, don't you?'

May didn't appear to hear Jamie. She scooped up several cans of spaghetti and balanced them carefully on top of an overflowing trolley. Her constant speech was unintelligible. Jamie turned back to look at Janet. 'What dose of chlorpromazine is in that syringe?'

'One hundred milligrams.'

'Hmm.' Jamie was watching May again. 'She's not a small woman, is she?'

'Stop *looking* at me!' May shrieked suddenly, staring at the lens of the security camera. A can of baked beans went wide of its target. Jamie grabbed Janet's arm and pulled her behind another shopper's abandoned trolley. He glanced at her.

'I don't think there's much hope of talking her out of this. If I get hold of her, do you think you can get an intramuscular injection in?'

Janet bit her lip. 'You wouldn't believe how many layers of clothing she wears. It takes her some time to expose skin and she's terrified of needles. She thinks they're after her blood.'

'They?'

Janet nodded. 'The same "they" that are watching her right now, I expect.'

'OK.' Jamie adjusted his crouch, ducking as another can passed overhead. His knee pressed against Janet's thigh. 'How about I sit on her and you try and find a site? Arm or leg?'

Janet almost giggled. 'I don't mind. You choose.'

Jamie's glance was quick. 'No—you choose.'

For a split second Janet forgot the predicament they

were in. She could feel the physical contact with Jamie. She could also feel the emotional contact. She still loved this man, she realised with dismay. How could she have ever thought otherwise? She couldn't begin to wonder what Jamie was thinking. His face had a guarded neutrality that advertised a deliberate distance. Perhaps he'd meant nothing more by the phrase than clarifying their present plan of action. It was the sight of two welcomingly robust ambulance officers advancing up the aisle that broke the moment. Janet blinked.

'A leg's going to be easiest, I think.'

With the extra assistance, it was surprisingly easy. The sedating effect of the drug was rapid and the crisis quickly over. May was bundled away for emergency psychiatric assessment. The supermarket manager was wringing his hands as he surveyed the chaos left behind. Janet and Jamie escaped.

'Is it Mondays?' Jamie queried as they neared Janet's car. 'Or is it something about me?'

Janet laughed. 'Must be something about you. I've never known St David's patients to behave so dramatically before. It'll probably be as dull as ditchwater as soon as you've gone.'

Jamie took hold of Janet's arm. 'I'm not going anywhere in a hurry,' he said quietly. He steered Janet away from the car. 'We need to talk,' he stated. 'Let's find somewhere to sit down for a minute.'

Janet had no choice but to comply. This had to happen and it may as well be now. At least they had some privacy. Janet shuddered to think how Oliver and Sophie might react when they became aware of the startling link between their practice nurse and the new locum. Jamie chose a park bench behind the supermarket which overlooked the river. A young couple sat on the grass nearby, holding hands. Janet adjusted her position on the bench to leave maximum space between her and Jamie. Jamie also shifted, leaning forward to place his elbows on his knees. To outward appearances he was enchanted by the view of the river and trees.

'I owe you an apology, Janet.'

Janet blinked. He was going to *apologise*? For what? Lying to her? Running off with Sharlene? Having a relationship with Janet in the first place and getting her pregnant?

'I shouldn't have said some of the things I accused you of on Friday. Our relationship is in the past and whatever reasons we had for a lack of trust are immaterial.'

'I wouldn't say that,' Janet said cautiously. None of it was immaterial now. She still loved him. If anything, it was more significant. If seven and a half years hadn't been enough to get over the way she felt about Jamie, what hope did she have for the rest of her life? 'Those reasons are precisely why we are sitting here now having this discussion,' she added.

'No,' Jamie said decisively. 'The reason we're sitting here now is that we have to discuss what happens in the future. Not the past. That part of our lives is long dead. It's the consequences that have to be dealt with.'

Janet felt cold despite the bright sunshine. It wasn't

dead at all. Not for her. It had all just been very effectively, and shockingly, resuscitated.

'I have dealt with the consequences,' she said flatly. 'I've coped fine until now. The boys are *my* children.'

Jamie finally turned his head and Janet could see his cold determination. 'They're also *my* children, Janet. If you want to make an issue about denying that, it would be quite possible to turn this into something nasty. Is that what you want? Legal intervention? DNA testing? Custody battles and access agreements?'

'You wouldn't do that,' Janet whispered in horror. 'Don't you have any idea how that could affect the boys?'

'Of course I do.' Jamie's gaze softened only fractionally. 'I'm their father, Janet. I have a right to be part of their lives. They have a right to know me.'

Janet felt her defences crumbling under the gaze. It wasn't just hostility she could see. Jamie looked uncertain. Hopeful. Even—possibly—a little afraid. Surprisingly, Janet felt more confident. Jamie wanted his sons to accept him. He wanted Janet's help. She felt her own expression softening, along with a resurgence of the wave of emotion she'd experienced in the supermarket. The boys would love their father. As much as she did.

'I'd like the boys to know you, Jamie,' Janet said gently. 'I'd like them to know that you are their father.'

Jamie didn't smile. He nodded seriously. 'Good. We're agreed, then.'

'Not quite.' Janet observed the deepening of the tiny lines around Jamie's eyes as he frowned. 'I want the boys to get to know you *before* they learn that you're their father. I don't want them told until I think they're ready.'

This time there was a long pause before Jamie nodded again. 'All right,' he said finally. 'But I want to get started as soon as possible. I'm only here for six weeks and we've wasted one of them already.'

'What do you suggest?' Janet ran her fingers through her curls as she tried to think. 'Shall we meet you somewhere? For a pizza or something?'

'No.' Jamie got to his feet. He checked his watch and smiled wryly. 'We'd better head back. Goodness knows what emergency is waiting for our attention now. It *is* still Monday.' He looked down at Janet, suddenly serious again. 'I want to meet the boys at home. Invite me to dinner.'

'OK.' Janet took a quick breath. How long would it take her to try and knock the house into a showpiece of maternal capabilities? 'What about Wednesday?'

'No,' Jamie said firmly. 'Tonight.'

Janet gulped. 'You want to come to dinner *tonight*?'

'Thank you.' The flash of Jamie's teeth as he grinned was unexpected. 'I'd love to accept your invitation.'

CHAPTER SEVEN

FATE was finally lending a helping hand.

The boys couldn't have chosen a better day to be behaving like angels. They'd gone straight to their bedroom when they'd arrived home, apparently only too keen to follow Janet's direction that they tidy their room. Janet had thrown herself into a whirlwind of domestic duties. Now the washing was done, the floor vacuumed, the table set and the dinner almost prepared. Adam and Rory had moved to the living room but, surprisingly, not to watch television. They were going to do their homework. If Janet hadn't been so grateful for the respite from demands for her attention, she would have been more than a little suspicious.

Now all she wanted was fifteen minutes to have a quick shower and change of clothes before their visitor arrived. Perhaps knowing that the stern Dr McFadden was coming for dinner had been enough to subdue the twins. It had had the opposite effect on Janet. She stood in front on her wardrobe five minutes later, towelling her hair dry and looking at the blue dress she'd made for Oliver's and Sophie's wedding. It was the prettiest item of clothing she possessed but Janet was dismayed that she wanted to wear it so badly. How could her feelings towards Jamie have reverted so dramatically? It only made the situation

124

more painful. Jamie wasn't coming here to see her. He was only interested in the twins.

Janet shut the wardrobe door and went to her chest of drawers. A clean pair of jeans, a cotton blouse and the dark blue jersey she'd knitted last winter would do. Comfortable, casual and definitely not intended to impress. Jamie wasn't haunted by any resurgence of past emotional depths and Janet had no intention of letting him know how she felt. He already held far too much power to influence the direction of her future happiness. Pleased with her choice of clothing, Janet ran a wide toothed comb through her curls and triumphantly suppressed the desire to touch up her make up. She ran downstairs just as the doorbell rang.

Jamie carried a bottle of wine. 'I couldn't think what to bring,' he said apologetically. 'I wanted to get something for the boys but...' His words trailed off awkwardly. The appeal in his face was touching. Jamie was understandably apprehensive about meeting his sons. Janet was in control of this situation. She could engineer an uncomfortable encounter that would make it extremely difficult for Jamie to build a relationship with his sons in the short time they had available. Or she could make it easy. Janet's lips curved into a gentle smile.

'Perfect choice,' she said, reaching to accept the bottle. 'Red wine is just what we need to go with the spaghetti Bolognese.' She caught Jamie's gaze again. 'Come through to the living room. They boys are busy doing their homework.'

The boys *were* busy, but their project looked nothing like the homework Janet had envisaged. Rory was attacking a cardboard apple carton with his Swiss army knife, hacking a round hole in one end. Adam lay on his stomach, attaching the cardboard centres of toilet rolls together with sticky tape.

'What on earth is going on?' Janet looked around the room in astonishment. Packaging from teabags, muesli bars, crackers and laundry powder cluttered the carpet. The newspaper which was normally stacked tidily ready for fire lighting requirements was a shredded heap to one side. Several saucers were lined up, one of which was brimming with what looked like rolled oats.

The boys straightened from their tasks with a speed that advertised guilt. Janet and Jamie found themselves looking down at tousled blond heads and bright little faces struggling to look innocent.

'Adam, Rory. This is…' Janet hesitated. How should she introduce Jamie? 'Your father' was out of the question. 'Dr McFadden' seemed ridiculously distant. 'This is…Jamie,' she told them. 'He's come for tea.'

'Hi, guys,' Jamie said casually.

The boys exchanged apprehensive glances. Janet frowned slightly. She knew the signal of brewing trouble. 'Where did you get all these boxes from?' she demanded.

'The pantry,' Adam confessed.

Janet's frown deepened. 'And what have you done with all the things that were inside the boxes?'

'They're still in the pantry,' Rory said virtuously. 'Don't worry, Mum.'

'Except for the soap powder,' Adam added. 'We put that in the bucket.'

Janet wasn't really listening. She was staring at Rory with an expression of dawning horror. The boys were sitting very still. Unnaturally immobile. Rory's jersey, however, was moving. A lump travelled from one shoulder towards the neckband. A pointed, whiskery nose appeared, followed by beady black eyes.

'*What*,' Janet enunciated very clearly, 'is *that*?'

Adam and Rory looked at each other. Adam watched the creature emerging from Rory's clothing and giggled nervously.

'It's a baby rat, Mum,' Rory said eagerly. 'Would you like to hold him?'

Jamie had an expectant grin on his face. His eyebrows were raised to maximum level, clearly anticipating a reaction from Janet that would involve her leaping onto the highest piece of furniture available, accompanied by a piercing vocal protest. Janet held out her hand calmly.

'You can hold mine, too,' Adam offered generously. 'When I get him out of my sleeve.' He shoved his hand down the neck of his own jersey.

Janet shook her head. 'One at a time, thanks.' She inspected the tiny black and white animal sitting on the palm of her hand. 'Very cute,' she acknowledged, 'but I don't remember saying that you were allowed to have one of Ben's rat's babies.'

'He gave us two,' Rory said appreciatively. 'He said they were twins—like us.'

Adam was eyeing Jamie. 'Would you like to hold *my* rat?' The challenge was subtle but unmistakable.

'Sure.' Jamie extended his hand. The rat took a running leap from Adam's hands, scampered up Jamie's arm and disappeared behind his collar. Jamie laughed.

'Tickles, doesn't it?' Adam was grinning happily.

'We're building them a maze,' Rory told Janet excitedly. 'With doors and tunnels. We're got all their food ready. See?' He pointed to the saucers. 'And we've made a bed out of newspapers.'

'Can we keep them, Mum?' Adam pleaded. 'We'll look after them. Please?'

Janet tickled the little rat in her hands. It sat up on its haunches, catching her finger with tiny front paws. Jamie was still tying to locate its sibling.

'*Please*, Mum,' the twins chorused.

Janet tilted her head. 'What do you think, Jamie?'

Jamie hauled his visitor from behind his shoulder by the tail. He looked questioningly at Janet and then at the desperately eager expressions of the boys.

'I don't know,' he said carefully. 'Do you think you can look after them?'

Adam and Rory nodded vigorously.

'Do you think it's going to make extra work for your mum?' Jamie's glance at the mess on the floor was pointed.

'We're going to tidy it all up,' Rory promised. 'We'll only get the boxes out when we want to play with them.'

'Have you got somewhere to keep them where they won't escape?'

'We've got the hutch the guinea pig had.' Adam nodded as he spoke. 'We're going to put the newspaper in there to keep them warm.'

'Hmm.' Jamie appeared reluctantly impressed. He smiled at Janet. 'What do *you* think, Janet?'

'I think it's time for dinner.' Janet handed the rat back to Rory. 'Let's see how well you tidy up after you put the rats away, and we'll talk about it again later.'

'Good move,' Jamie said approvingly when he returned to the kitchen, having been to the bathroom to wash his hands. 'Things are getting tidied up remarkably fast. Will you let them keep the rats?'

'I suppose so.' Janet was adding dried pasta to the pot of boiling water. 'It might stop them begging for a dog for a while longer.'

'Why don't you want a dog?'

'It's not that I don't want one.' Janet opened a drawer and searched for a corkscrew. 'It's simply not practical.' She handed the corkscrew to Jamie. 'Could you open the wine, please? I'd better go and make sure those children have scrubbed their hands.'

Adam and Rory raced into the kitchen minutes later. They sat down on either side of the table and watched Janet draining the spaghetti.

'Cool!' Rory announced. 'Worms for tea.'

'That's enough,' Janet reprimanded him. 'Do sit down, Jamie—we're almost ready.'

Jamie sat down at one end of the table. Janet sat at the other, having served their meals. Adam and Rory were making faces at each other, trying not to laugh, as they attacked the uncooperative food with their forks. Rory picked up the end of a long piece of pasta, holding it up in his fingers and wiggling it. Adam collapsed in giggles.

'That's *enough*!' Janet warned sharply. She glanced apprehensively at Jamie. Did teaching table manners figure importantly in the catalogue of maternal skills? Jamie was having difficulty keeping a straight face. The eye contact with Janet was too much for him and he laughed.

'I remember my mother telling me off for calling spaghetti worms,' he confessed. 'I'd forgotten about it until now.'

Adam and Rory looked at him admiringly. 'Did your mother make you eat toenails, too?'

Jamie's glance appealed to Janet for assistance. She laughed. 'They don't like the oat husks in their porridge,' she explained. 'They have it for breakfast every day.'

'I did, too,' Jamie told the boys. 'It's the best breakfast in the world. Everybody eats it in Scotland, where I come from.'

'Our mum comes from Scotland,' Rory announced importantly.

'I know.' Jamie nodded agreement.

'Our dad does, too,' Adam added. 'That's where he lives.'

'Is it?' Jamie's forkful of spaghetti halted in midair. He caught Janet's eye. She looked away quickly.

'Was your porridge full of toenails?' Rory asked with interest. 'Did you have to spit them out?'

'Uh…' Jamie was still looking at Adam. 'I don't remember.'

'We do,' Adam confided. 'When Mum's not look-ing.'

'Who gets the most?' Jamie turned his attention back to his plate.

'I do,' Rory said.

'No—*I* do,' Adam contradicted.

'How many do you get on average, then?' Jamie enquired.

'What's average?'

Janet ate quietly, listening to Jamie explain how to calculate an average. The boys were listening atten-tively. Part of Janet sat back, observing the scene. The small table had someone on each side. A complete set. A real family. Janet put her fork down hurriedly. 'Who's ready for ice cream?'

'Me!' the twins shouted in gleeful unison.

'Me, too,' Jamie added. 'That was great. Thanks very much, Janet.' His gaze was as warmly apprecia-tive as his tone. He was referring to more than the meal.

'You're welcome.' Janet's smile felt a little tight. 'You'll have to come back again soon.'

Jamie left when the twins were shuttled off to the bathroom to get ready for bed. Janet refused his offer to help with the dishes. Being a visitor was one thing. She wasn't ready for his inclusion in the more inti-mate domestic routine of her household.

It was easier at work. Jamie made a point of talking to the twins when they arrived to wait for Janet after school the next afternoon. They discussed the dietary requirements of juvenile rodents. On Wednesday afternoon Janet saw the boys disappearing into Jamie's consulting room.

'They asked if they could have a go on the computer,' he explained as he came out for his next patient. 'I thought I could see Mrs Simpson in the side room.'

Janet went looking for them half an hour later when she was ready to go home. She could hear Rory's piping voice through the open door.

'We were going to get our own computer for our birthday,' he was saying sadly. 'But we burnt down Mrs Carpenter's shed by mistake.'

'Is not getting a computer your punishment, then?'

Janet paused outside the door at the sound of Jamie's voice.

'Not really.' Adam sounded ready to defend his mother's methods of discipline. 'It's just that Mum saved up for a whole year for the deposit and now she has to give the money to Mrs Carpenter instead.'

'Oh.' Jamie sounded understanding. 'That's a shame.'

'Maybe we'll get a PlayStation instead,' Rory said matter-of-factly. 'They're cheaper.'

Janet bustled into the room as though she hadn't paused in her journey. 'Time to go home, boys.'

'Can Jamie come for tea again?' Adam asked.

'Not tonight,' Janet said, a little too quickly.

'Tomorrow?' Rory suggested.

Janet hesitated. Adam's face was screwing itself into persuasive lines. '*Please*, Mum? We want to show him the maze. It's all finished now.'

'I'd like to see that,' Jamie said enthusiastically.

He was watching Janet carefully, adding yet another set of brown eyes, awaiting a decision.

'OK,' Janet agreed. 'Tomorrow's fine.'

Jamie arrived earlier on Thursday evening. Janet hadn't even started the meal preparations. She looked at the familiar cardboard containers Jamie was holding.

'Was the spaghetti that bad?' she asked with mock indignation. 'You've come prepared for the worst tonight.'

Jamie grinned. 'I raided your cupboard. I thought they might be a useful addition to the maze.'

Janet shook her head. 'Go on, then. Add to the mess. Now that the maze is built it can't be tidied away apparently. The connections would break.'

Janet worked in the kitchen for half an hour, peacefully uninterrupted. She'd splashed out a bit tonight, roasting a chicken and vegetables. She hoped the boys wouldn't reveal that this dinner was normally reserved for special occasions. Ready to call everyone together for the meal, Janet found them all lying on the living room floor. Jamie had a rat on his head. Rory held a cardboard tube that had a pink tail emerging from one end. They barely noticed Janet's entrance. An in-depth discussion of football was in progress.

'The Crusaders always win,' Adam said proudly. 'They're the best.'

'The Highlanders are pretty good, too,' Janet reminded him. 'They might even win the final. Now put those rats away and go and wash your hands. All of you.'

Jamie was the first to comply. The twins raced him to the door.

'We've got the Crusaders music on a tape,' Rory told Jamie excitedly. 'Would you like to hear it?'

'Sure,' Jamie agreed. 'After you've put Popeye and Olive away.'

'Popeye and Olive?' Janet queried as soon as Jamie reached the kitchen.

'They needed names,' Jamie said seriously. 'And their eyes kind of stick out, don't they?'

Janet turned off the oven. 'I hope you're not telling me we've got a male and a female rat.'

Jamie grinned. 'Hadn't you noticed?'

Janet groaned. 'I hadn't looked.' She lifted the chicken onto the carving dish. 'I hope they're not going to…'

Jamie was standing close beside her. He reached for the carving knife on the bench, his arm brushing Janet's. He stopped suddenly.

'Going to what, Janet?' he asked softly. 'Make babies?' Janet could feel his breath on the side of her neck. 'Like we did?'

Janet turned her head slowly and raised her glance. She met the look in Jamie's eyes and her mouth went dry. A shaft of desire speared her abdomen with an exquisite pain.

'Chicken!' Rory shouted behind her elbow. 'Cool!'

'It's not even our birthday,' Adam crowed. 'Can I have a drumstick?'

'Can I have one, too?' Rory was holding their small cassette player. 'We've brought the Crusaders' song for you, Jamie.'

Jamie dragged his eyes away from Janet's. 'Why don't you play it,' he suggested, 'while I find you a drumstick each?' He grinned at the boys. 'It's just as well a chicken's got two legs, isn't it?'

'Conquest of Paradise' had been played a total of six times by the end of the meal. Jamie had been suitably impressed.

'Stirring stuff,' he pronounced. 'I hope Mr Collins was right. Definitely preferable to bright lights and tunnels.'

'Who's Mr Collins?' Rory asked.

'A Crusaders fan,' Janet told them. 'If you've finished your dinner you'd better go and do your homework. I haven't seen a reading book all week.'

Adam and Rory both made disgusted faces. Jamie looked surprised. 'Don't you like reading?'

The boys were silent. Janet had to find something to say to break the uncomfortable silence.

'The boys aren't finding reading very easy at the moment,' she said casually. 'We're working on it.'

'It's because we're twins,' Adam said unexpectedly.

'Really?' Jamie sounded intrigued. 'How does that work?'

'Ben says there was only one brain and so we got half each,' Rory explained. 'That's why we're dumb.'

Janet bit her lip. She'd never heard that particular bit of peer wisdom. How was she going to start building the boys' confidence in their abilities if they believed a notion like that?

'I don't believe you for a minute,' Jamie said easily. 'Can I see your reading books?'

Janet did the dishes alone again. She also put the washing on, tidied the twins' bunk beds and ran a bath for them. They still hadn't emerged from the living room. Again, Janet found the three of them lying on their stomachs on the floor, propped up on their elbows. Jamie had a book open under his nose.

'C and h,' he was saying. 'Ch.' What's something you could put in a sandwich that starts like that?'

'Chips,' Adam offered.

'Chocolate.' Rory giggled.

'What else?'

The twins were clearly engrossed. Janet sat quietly on the arm of the couch. Where had Jamie learned how to teach reading?

'Chops,' Adam decided.

'Chicken,' Rory said hopefully.

'OK, look at the picture,' Jamie directed. The boys leaned closer, one of either side of Jamie. The three heads were virtually touching. Golden blond curls meeting the darker waves of Jamie's hair. It was the colour their hair would turn as they got older. Hints of the darker brown were already coming through. Janet felt a poignant stab at the reminder of how quickly the boys were growing and changing. She saw their suddenly eager faces as they both looked up into the face of the man lying between them.

'Cheese!' they both said triumphantly.

'Very good!' Jamie congratulated them. 'Well done. I'm proud of you.'

'I'm proud of you, too,' Janet said. Jamie and the boys looked up in surprise. 'Now it's time for a bath and bed.'

'Aw, Mum. Can't we do some more reading with Jamie? Please?'

'It's fun,' Adam added.

'We'll do some more next time,' Jamie said. 'You heard what your mum said. Now, scoot!'

The boys scooted. Jamie climbed to his feet and looked down at Janet, still perched on the arm of the couch.

'They're certainly not dumb,' he told her. 'They're a bright little pair.'

'That's what Josh said. He couldn't believe how fast they picked things up on his computer. I don't know why they're having trouble with reading.'

Jamie shrugged. 'Maybe it's too slow to be interesting.' He held Janet's gaze. 'They should have a computer. There must be great software around to help with reading skills. The combination might be just what they need to get started.'

Janet stood up. 'I'm going to get them a computer,' she said defensively.

'When you can afford it.' Jamie quirked an eyebrow. 'When will that be, Janet?'

'As soon as possible,' Janet responded stiffly.

'They need it right now.'

'Well, they can't have it right now.' Janet glared at Jamie. 'Not everyone gets what they want or need precisely when they want or need it, you know.'

'They could have it now,' Jamie said evenly. 'I could buy them a computer.'

'I'm sure you could,' Janet said bitterly. 'I'm sure you can afford a lot of things I can't. You could buy the boys' love with no trouble at all.'

'Is that what you think I want to do?'

Janet shrugged. 'It's a lot quicker than earning it. You won't have to spend years making do and keeping rules. Putting up with the noise and mess, sorting out the arguments and nursing them through all the illnesses. I've done all that. By myself.'

Jamie's face tightened. 'And whose fault was that, Janet? Did you give me any choice?'

Janet was silent. She could see Jamie's anger gathering and wished it wasn't too late to take back what she'd said.

'The only reason I wasn't there is because of your stubbornness. Your lies.' Jamie's fists were clenched. 'I've missed knowing my children as babies. Watching them grow into children. I've missed their first teeth, their first steps, their first words. It's unforgivable, Janet.'

Janet remained mute. What could she possibly say in her own defence? She'd felt the sadness of being reminded how fast her children were growing and changing only minutes before and she hadn't missed any of the milestones Jamie was so aware of.

'We agreed to put the past behind us so I'm trying very hard not to hold what I've missed against you,' Jamie said with an obvious effort at self-control. 'I'm not going to let it interfere with the relationship I can have with my sons now. You owe it to me to stand back. You've got no right to deny Adam and Rory what I can offer them because of your jealousy.'

'I'm *not* jealous,' Janet protested fiercely.

'Yes, you are.' Jamie eyed her impassively. 'You always were. If you hadn't been, I might have been here to earn the love of my children. I might not be standing here realising just how important what I've missed was. How nothing could ever make up for that loss.'

Janet had to look away. The bitter accusation was, in part, justified. She wanted to apologise—to say she understood—but the words would trivialise the depth of the emotions involved. Saying sorry wouldn't make things right. She could never make things completely right. But she could make a start.

'Maybe you could wait until their birthday to give them a computer,' she suggested quietly. 'It's only a month away. Otherwise they might wonder why they're getting such a big present.'

'Don't you think it's time to tell them the real reason?'

'No.' Janet turned a frightened gaze towards Jamie. 'Not yet.'

'Why not?'

'Because…because they're not ready.'

'You mean *you're* not ready.'

'They've only just met you,' Janet said slowly. 'They really like you. But I don't know how they'll react to the truth. They might…they might feel threatened.'

Jamie's gaze hadn't left Janet's face. 'You mean *you* feel threatened,' he said softly. His face relaxed a little. 'All right. We'll wait a little longer.' Jamie cleared his throat. 'I'd like to take the boys out on Saturday. To spend some time alone with them.'

Janet nodded. That was the usual sort of access

arrangement between estranged parents. She could handle it.

'Any suggestions of a good place to take them?'

'I'm sure the boys will have plenty of ideas. Why don't you go up and ask them?'

'Aren't they in the bath?'

'It's time they got out.' Janet bent to pick the instructional reading book up from the floor. 'Do the parent thing and make them clean their teeth and get into bed.' She straightened and found Jamie looking at her with a strange expression. Then he smiled. A small, rather pleased smile.

'Sure.' The smile faded, making him look very serious. 'I'll do the parent thing.'

CHAPTER EIGHT

JANET opened the autoclave hatch cautiously.

Her fingers were well away from the escaping steam. Jamie nodded approvingly. 'See? If you're not in too much of a hurry, you won't get hurt.'

Janet smiled sweetly. 'I'm sure I'll acquire the necessary wisdom by the time I reach your advanced years, Jamie McFadden.'

'I'm only five years older than you,' Jamie protested mildly. 'Thirty-five is hardly geriatric.' He eyed the tray Janet was setting out. 'Has our patient arrived yet?'

'No.' Janet reached for a pack of dressings. 'But Constance is worth waiting for. You'll love her.'

'I suppose she can be forgiven for not moving at the speed of light. How old is she again?'

Janet grinned. 'Ninety-eight. Her daughter is driving her in.'

Jamie raised an eyebrow. 'How old is her daughter?'

'Well into her seventies. She's just a youngster.'

'Nice to have some people's genes,' Jamie commented. 'Do you think this ulcer's going to be much of a problem?'

'Hard to tell until we remove the callus,' Janet said. 'Her diabetes is quite well controlled but she has diminished pulses and sensation in both feet. I hope the blood supply will be adequate for reasonably fast healing.'

'Might slow her down a wee bit more for a while.' Jamie was looking amused. 'I can't wait to meet her.'

Janet selected a bottle of hydrogen peroxide from her cupboard. 'We're all set. I'll call you when Constance arrives if you like.'

'I'm not busy.' Jamie's face brightened. 'How were the boys this morning?'

'Great.' Janet smiled.

'Did they eat their porridge?'

'They won't consider eating anything else now. It's a competition to see who gets the highest average of toenails before you visit again. I have to keep a chart on the breakfast table and they mark each one and then count them up at the end. Rory asked for a second helping this morning.'

Jamie looked pleased. 'That'll do them good. Nothing wrong with lots of porridge.'

'It's doing their maths skills some good at the same time.' Janet caught Jamie's eye. 'You're a natural, Jamie.'

'A natural what?'

'Parent. You seem to know the right thing to do and say without even trying.' Janet tried not to sound resentful. She'd never had anybody to tell her whether or not she'd been doing a great job in the early years of being a mother. She'd learned her parenting skills the hard way—by trial and error.

Jamie straightened proudly. 'Do you think so?'

Janet looked at Jamie again. Giving the praise had been worthwhile. She could see the pleasure she had clearly given him. 'I know so. I may not be as old and wise as you, but I've had a bit more practice at the parent thing.'

Jamie nodded. Then he smiled rather poignantly. 'I had no idea how well I was doing.' He reached out and touched her hand. 'Thanks for that, Janna.'

Janna. No one else had ever used that diminutive of her name. And Jamie hadn't used it since he'd reappeared in her life. It was more than friendly. The intimacy of the private name curled around Janet's abdomen and squeezed deliciously. Jamie's hand was still touching hers and she couldn't look away. If she turned her hand over, she could return the touch. She wanted to return it—and more.

'You're welcome,' she said softly. 'And it's true. You've only known the boys for a couple of weeks. They think you're wonderful.'

'They're wonderful kids. You've done a great job.'

'Thanks.' Janet's hand turned and she squeezed Jamie's fingers gently.

'They talk about you all the time,' Jamie added. He didn't try and remove his hand. 'Except when they're talking about how much they want a dog.'

Janet laughed. 'They can be very persistent when they've set their hearts on something. I'll bet you hear about it every time you take them out.'

'Sure do.' The pressure of Jamie's hand enclosing hers increased as he grinned. 'On the trip to Orana Park the wolves looked like dogs. At the Antarctic Centre they wouldn't leave the husky exhibit. Even the movie I took them to was a dog story.' Jamie's tone became serious. 'They should have a dog, Janet. It would be good for them.'

Janet pulled her hand free. The moment of closeness had gone. She could sense potential criticism of her parenting. 'We couldn't possibly keep a dog. I work long hours. It wouldn't be fair.'

'So stop working long hours. If you only worked part time, you could be home for the boys after school and in the holidays *and* you could let them have a dog.'

'I can't afford that.'

'You can now.' Jamie's stare was intent. 'I can help.'

'I don't want your money,' Janet said sharply. 'I'm not going to lose my independence. How long do you think I could rely on you, Jamie? What happens when a better offer comes up and you walk away? Where would that leave us?'

'I'm not going to walk away,' Jamie said impatiently. 'Maybe you should learn to trust me.'

'Oh?' Janet stepped back, her face tense. 'Like last time, you mean?'

Jamie looked angry now. 'Yes, like last time,' he said menacingly. 'If you hadn't been so bloody—' He broke off as Sandy knocked on the half-open door. She was grinning.

'Constance Purdie is here,' she announced. 'Shall I bring her through?'

'Yes, please.' Janet nodded quickly. She didn't want to hear what Jamie had been about to say. What further blame he was going to lay at her feet. He still seemed to consider their break-up to have been her fault. What a nerve! They both needed to step back and cool off before their acrimony made it impossible for them to work together.

Constance Purdie was tiny, only a little over five feet tall. She had a round face and tightly permed white hair. She walked with only the aid of a walking stick. Her daughter, Hope, had never married and was a younger version of her mother. Her permed hair was grey instead of white and as yet, she needed no help in walking.

Jamie was smiling again. 'I don't believe this is your daughter, Mrs Purdie,' he said. 'You look like sisters.'

Constance Purdie beamed at Jamie. 'You're a very charming young man,' she announced. 'Are you married?'

'Mother!' Hope Purdie remonstrated.

'It's all right, dear.' Constance allowed Janet to remove her jacket and help her onto the bed. 'He's too young for you. I was thinking more about wee Janet here.'

Janet smiled, shaking her head. 'Let's get these shoes off, Constance. And your stockings.'

'I don't know why you're making such a fuss about my feet, dear. They don't hurt a bit.'

'Ulcers can get nasty if they're not looked after properly.' Jamie was putting on a pair of surgical gloves. 'And Janet tells me you're a very special patient, Mrs Purdie.'

'You can call me Constance,' she told him. 'And what's your name, dear?'

'Oh, I'm sorry,' Janet apologised. 'This is Dr Jamie McFadden. He's filling in for us while Josh is away.'

'Where's Dr Cooper?'

'He's on his honeymoon, Mother. I've told you that already. Several times.' Hope Purdie had settled herself on the chair at the foot of the bed.

'Don't snap at me, child,' Constance reprimanded her daughter. 'I'm not senile yet.' She turned an alert gaze on Janet. 'It's about time you had a honeymoon yourself, Janet Muir. What's wrong with this young man? Looks like a strapping lad to me.'

'Mother!'

'Oh, all right.' Constance tutted irritably. 'I just can't understand you girls these days. So fussy! Look at my Hope here. It's going to be too late for her if she doesn't get a wriggle on.'

Jamie caught Janet's eye. She could see the amusement bubbling in his face. Neither of them dared look directly at Hope who was sending distinctly mutinous messages with her body language. A wriggle of any sort seemed highly unlikely.

'Can you feel this at all, Constance?' Jamie was prodding the sole of the old lady's foot with a disposable toothpick.

'Can't feel a thing,' Constance assured him. 'I told you it was nothing that needed a fuss.'

'Janet was quite right to make this appointment for you,' Jamie told Constance. 'This is quite a big callus and it has an ulcer developing underneath. We need to remove the hard skin on top, clean things up and then put a dressing on it.' Jamie took the tweezers

Janet was holding. 'This should be completely pain-
less.'

Jamie worked quickly, removing the dead skin and
debris, exposing a surprisingly large ulcerated area.
'We'll flush this with saline,' he told Janet, 'and then
give it a fizz with some hydrogen peroxide and flush
it again before we put a dressing on.' He glanced at
the shoes lying beside the bed. 'You're going to need
some footwear that will help protect your feet,' he
told Constance. 'Something with plenty of toe room,
a shock-absorbing sole and laces so you can adjust
the level of support. Trainers are ideal.'

'Trainers? You mean those stripy things the runners
wear?'

'Aye.' Jamie nodded. He watched as Janet flushed
the ulcerated area with the second dose of saline and
nodded again approvingly. 'Nice and clean. Let's put
on an impregnated dressing and some Tegaderm. It'll
need a dressing change every two to three days for a
while.'

'I'd like some of those shoes,' Constance announced. 'I think we'd better go shopping, Hope.'

'Not today, Mother.'

'No time like the present.' Constance wagged her
head and smiled at Jamie. 'At my age, you have to
get on with things. If you wait it might just turn out
to be too late.'

'Absolutely,' Jamie agreed. He looked at Janet and
winked. She smiled back, grateful that the tension between them had evaporated. Constance Purdie and her
daughter left a short time later, and Jamie shook his
head admiringly. 'That was a bit of a treat.' He looked

at Janet questioningly. 'Do you suppose she really thinks there's still time to get Hope married off?'

'Age is relative, I guess.' Janet smiled. 'I hope I'm still that enthusiastic about life when I'm ninety-eight.'

'I hope I am when I'm thirty-eight.' Jamie grinned. 'Right now I'd like to put my feet up and have a cup of tea. Have you got time for a break?'

'I'd love one.' Janet nodded.

'Good.' Jamie led the way to the staffroom. 'You can tell me about another place I can take the boys to on the weekend.'

Janet tried to think as she filled the jug and put it on to boil. It had been two weeks since Jamie had asked to have time out with the boys by himself. Two weekends where they'd spent a whole day out together. Jamie had been to the house for dinner on another occasion and had taken Janet and the boys out to a pizza restaurant only two nights previously. The boys were loving it but had been suspicious on the first occasion. Janet had made sure they'd been dressed in clean clothes and had brushed their teeth.

'Why aren't you coming?' Adam queried anxiously.

'Because Jamie wants to spend some time just with you and Rory.'

'Why?'

'He likes you,' Janet said casually. 'Come here, I need to brush your hair again.'

'Dennis never took us anywhere,' Adam reminded her.

'Dennis was a dork,' Rory stated. Janet ignored the giggles.

'Jamie's not a dork,' Adam said decisively.

'No.' Rory was quick to agree. 'Jamie's cool.'

'So you're happy about it, then?' Janet asked.

'About what?'

'Going out with Jamie. Without me.'

'Where are we going?'

'Orana Park.'

The boys nudged each other gleefully. 'Awesome!'

They didn't even ask if Janet was going with them the next time, and Janet was startled by her reaction to seeing them drive off. She recognised the jealousy she felt and was dismayed. Had Jamie been right all along and she just had a jealous and suspicious nature? What was even more disturbing was that the jealousy wasn't directed at Jamie for having the pleasure of a special outing with the boys. She felt jealous of her sons having the time alone with Jamie.

'That tea is going to be completely stewed.'

Janet jumped. 'Och, sorry. I was miles away.'

'So, have you thought of somewhere for us to go?'

'There's the Crusaders game coming up. If you're lucky you might be able to get tickets.'

'That's not for a couple of weeks.'

'You don't have to go anywhere special.' Janet poured the tea carefully. 'They're quite happy to kick a ball around the park or even stay home. They want to try building a wooden maze for the rats. The cardboard one's falling to bits.' Janet handed Jamie the sugar bowl. 'And they're keen to finish the story you all started writing the other night in the restaurant.'

'"The Poisonous Pizza"?' Jamie grinned. 'That was great fun.'

'They want to write it down.' Janet hesitated. 'It's just the sort of thing the remedial reading people encourage.' She sipped at her tea, still standing beside the bench. 'I had a call from the headmistress of their school yesterday. She wanted me to know how well the boys are doing at the moment. She said there's been a huge difference in the last couple of weeks.'

'Is that right?' Jamie blinked in surprise. 'You don't think that's got anything to do with me, do you?'

Janet nodded slowly. 'I suspect it has everything to do with you, Jamie. Have you noticed they've even started talking with a Scottish accent?'

'No.' Jamie looked delighted. '*Have* they?'

'Aye.'

Jamie laughed. 'Do you listen to yourself, then?'

'I don't have much of an accent any more.'

'Nonsense. Some things you can never get rid of. You sound exactly the same as the day I met you, Janna.'

Janet put her mug down on the bench. No, some things you could never get rid of. Like the way that name made her feel. Like the way she felt about Jamie McFadden.

'It's about time we told the boys, isn't it?' Jamie asked softly. 'I mean, the truth about me.'

'No. Not yet.' Janet's hand bumped her mug and some tea slopped over the side. She reached hastily for the dishcloth. 'As you just told me, if you don't do things in too much of a hurry, then you don't get hurt.'

'I prefer Constance's philosophy,' Jamie countered. 'If you wait, it might just turn out to be too late. I want to tell them,' he said firmly. 'Soon.'

'No!' Janet tipped the rest of her tea into the sink. 'I don't want to talk about it.'

'We have to talk about it,' Jamie said grimly.

'Not right now. I've got work to do.'

'Tonight, then.'

'No.'

Jamie caught Janet's arm. 'The boys are going to be told. If you won't even talk about how and when, I'll just go ahead and do it my way. Is that what you want?'

'No,' Janet whispered. 'You know it isn't.'

'Then we'll talk,' Jamie said coolly. 'Tonight.'

Tonight. The word hung over Janet for the rest of the day. She tried hard to keep up her normal level of enthusiasm but even the patients seemed to want to make life more difficult. Like Mrs Terence, who came in for her next pack of nicotine replacement patches and pep talk and promptly burst into tears.

'I've started smoking again,' she sobbed. 'I can't do this. I'm a complete failure.'

Janet handed over the box of tissues and drew her chair closer. 'One little setback isn't a failure, Mrs Terence. You've been doing so well. You *can* win.'

'No.' Mrs Terence blew her nose vigorously. 'It was one little setback last week. On Monday I had three and today I've already had five. I feel so depressed about failing I just *have* to smoke.'

'It's not the end of the world,' Janet said sooth-ingly. 'And it doesn't mean you're never going to be able to stop. It just means starting again.'

'I can't,' her patient moaned. 'Truly—I can't face it.'

'It doesn't have to be today,' Janet said calmly. 'You need to feel ready and choose another time. Then we'll start again. You might find you understand your difficulties better after this. It'll make you stronger next time. Better prepared.'

Mrs Terence dabbed at her eyes. 'Maybe I should try acupuncture instead. Or hypnosis. That might be easier.'

'It's never going to be easy,' Janet warned. 'All these methods simply help. Most people find the patches work better than anything else. You have to be ready, though. And you have to really want to give up.'

'I do, I do. I *hate* myself for smoking,' Mrs Terence said fervently.

'Let me know when you're ready to try again,' Janet told her. 'Don't leave it too long.'

'No, I won't. Thank you, Janet.' Mrs Terence smiled a little shakily as she left.

Mr Courtney came in next, accompanied by his wife. They were both large people but it was Mr Courtney's blood test that indicated a high cholesterol level. Oliver wanted to try some dietary intervention as a first response. Janet's initial queries about the Courtney's dietary habits indicated that she had an-other uphill battle on her hands.

'Fruit?' Mrs Courtney echoed. 'The only way

Bernie eats fruit is if it's cooked in a crumble and has whipped cream on top.'

Bernard Courtney licked his lips involuntarily. Janet got up to retrieve some pamphlets from her desk. 'There are lots of good ideas for reducing saturated fats in these,' she explained. 'You don't have to do it all at once. One small change every week is enough. Like using a polyunsaturated margarine instead of butter. Or removing all the visible fat from meat and the skin from chicken.'

'The skin's the best part,' Mr Courtney protested. Janet glanced out of her window as she handed each of the Courtneys a pamphlet. Mrs Terence was standing outside on the footpath, lighting a cigarette. Janet sighed inwardly and sat down.

'Let's go over these ideas,' she suggested, 'and we can talk about the best way to get started.'

The cases that followed the Courtneys fortunately needed little in the way of counselling. Janet checked peak-flow readings for asthmatic patients, took blood tests and pressures, gave injections and changed dressings. Between patients she was in and out of the main office and the side room, but she deliberately kept contact with her colleagues brief.

Sandy was doing her job brilliantly and needed little assistance. Sophie was coping well enough but was still subdued and looked pale. Oliver and Jamie were positively cheerful. They were chatting together in Oliver's office when Janet went to get a glass of water from the staffroom. She heard Jamie laugh as she passed the door and the sound made her flinch. Perhaps he was actually looking forward to their meeting tonight. He had stepped firmly into the lives of Janet and her sons and was now in a position to take control.

Jamie was coming out of Oliver's room as Janet made her return journey.

'Seven o'clock,' he told her quietly. 'You don't have to feed me tonight.'

'The boys go to bed at 7.30,' Janet reminded him.

'I know.' Jamie's gaze locked with hers. 'It's *you* I'm coming to talk to, Janet.'

Adam and Rory had no intention of leaving their mother alone with Jamie. They bounced around in their pyjamas and bare feet.

'Let's do the story,' they begged Jamie. 'About the pizza. Please!'

Jamie looked at Janet. The boys looked at Janet. She shook her head in defeat. 'Ten minutes,' she said sternly. 'And then it's time for bed.'

They sat at the kitchen table while Janet made sandwiches for the lunch-boxes.

'Let's do a story about a sandwich,' Jamie suggested. 'Instead of pizza. Like that reading book you showed me.'

'OK.' Adam and Rory looked eager. 'What's the first letter?'

'P.'

'Peas,' Rory said quickly.

'Potatoes,' Adam added.

'Porridge!' Adam shouted.

Jamie was scribbling the words down on a large

sheet of paper. 'Two letters this time,' he announced.
'C and h. Do you remember what sound that makes?'

'Ch,' the twins told him proudly.

'Chocolate,' Rory offered.

'Chips,' Adam put in.

'Cheese,' Janet called. She waved the slice she was
about to lay on the bread.

Jamie and the boys all glanced up, appearing surprised at her uninvited suggestion. Or was the thought
of including her in the game the surprise? Janet
smiled almost shyly and turned quickly back to her
task. She didn't have to be a part of it. There were
plenty of things she should be doing—like sorting the
washing she'd taken down from the line hours ago.
Janet hunted for the matching socks. The laundry was
out of sight from the kitchen table but she could still
hear the game clearly. The boys showed no signs of
waning enthusiasm as Jamie coached them through
the sounds of several more consonants.

'We'll have to put it together,' he said finally. 'It's
time you boys went to bed.' There was a short silence
and then Jamie cleared his throat. 'Adam and Rory
were hungry,' he said.

'They were *very* hungry,' Rory broke in.

'Write that bit down, Jamie,' Adam instructed.
'What's next?'

Jamie pointed to the words on the paper. 'They
decided to make a sandwich,' he read. 'Adam found
the butter, a knife and some bread. Rory started looking for something to spread.'

The twins giggled.

'Shall we have chocolate and cheese, or big blue berries or pickles and porridge and peas?'

The boys shrieked with laughter. Janet shot out of the laundry. 'OK, settle down.'

'That's as far as we've got anyway,' Jamie said placatingly. 'Off to bed, boys. We'll finish our story another time.'

'Will you come up and tuck us in, Jamie?'

The boys trailed upstairs, still giggling. Janet heard them chanting from the bathroom.

'Adam and Rory were hungry. They were *ve-ery* hungry.'

There were more giggles and muted thumps from the bedroom a short time later.

'Shall we have chocolate and cheese?'

'Yes!' shouted Adam.

'Or big blue berries?'

'No!' shouted Rory.

'Or pickles and porridge and peas?'

'*Yuck!*' the twins yelled happily. 'Double yuck!'

The noise level had subsided by the time Jamie came downstairs. Janet went up to kiss the boys good-night and found them virtually asleep. For the first time ever, Janet wished they weren't quite so good at going to sleep. Returning to the kitchen, she procrastinated as long as she could, tidying the kitchen bench, making a pot of tea and finally lugging the laundry basket into place on the kitchen table. Jamie sat, watching her patiently.

'Sit down, Janet,' he said eventually. 'Your tea's getting cold.'

Janet kept her eyes on the washing basket. 'I just

need to find some clean underwear for the boys. If I don't get organised now, it's chaos in the morning.' She pulled several T-shirts from the top of the pile.

Jamie sighed. He leaned back in his chair and fixed Janet with a very direct look. 'You can't make this go away, Janet. I think you'd better explain exactly why you don't want the boys told about me yet.'

'Because...' Janet smoothed a T-shirt against her body, before folding it hurriedly. 'Because they've become very attached to you.'

'All the *more* reason for telling them, I would have thought.' Jamie sounded puzzled.

Janet pulled a pair of jeans from the basket and stretched the legs. 'It's only two weeks until Josh and Toni come back. You won't be working at St David's any more. You'll probably decide to move on. The boys will be upset.' Janet abandoned the jeans and fished out a sock. She stared at the basket. 'They'd be devastated if they knew you were their father and you still went away.' Janet tried to keep her voice steady. The boys wouldn't be the only ones who would be devastated. How could this be happening to her? *Again.*

'I love these children, Janet,' Jamie said quietly. 'My commitment to them won't change—wherever I am.'

Janet screwed the sock up in her hand. She bit her lip and blinked hard, fighting back tears. 'What if you go back to Scotland? Am I going to have to pack my sons off in the holidays and send them to the other side of the world?' She drew in a ragged breath. 'How will I ever know whether I can really trust you to send them back?'

'The same way I'd know I could trust you to send them to me.'

Janet's tears overflowed uncontrollably as she turned a desperate gaze towards Jamie. 'I admit I was wrong, Jamie. I should have tried harder to let you know I was pregnant. I shouldn't have kept you apart from your children. And maybe…maybe…' Janet stifled a sob and looked away from Jamie's sombre face. 'Maybe I deserve to be punished. But not this, Jamie. Please. Adam and Rory are all I have. It's too…' Janet covered her face with her hands, muffling her words.

Jamie's chair scraped on the floor as he pushed it back roughly. Janet felt strong arms encircle her. She was pulled firmly against Jamie's chest. She could feel his heart beating steadily, could feel the soothing hand stroking her head as she pressed her face into his shoulder. She could hear the deep, gentle rumble of Jamie's voice.

'I'm not trying to punish you, Janet. I don't want to hurt you *or* the boys. I'll never do that. Believe me.'

Janet raised her head slowly. She wanted to believe it so badly. The raw emotion she saw in Jamie's face stilled her fears. She *did* believe it. Maybe everything *had* been her fault. How could she have ever doubted this man? Or doubted the strength of their love.

'Trust me, Janna,' Jamie said softly.

'I will,' Janet whispered. 'I do trust you, Jamie. We'll tell the boys. Soon.'

Janet saw the relief and joy in Jamie's eyes. Then his grip tightened as he pulled her swiftly closer again. 'Thank you,' he whispered. 'Thank you.'

Jamie's cheek was pressed against Janet's curls. She closed her eyes as she felt his head turn and his lips brushed her forehead. She heard her name spoken almost as a groan.

'Oh, *Janna.*'

Janet lifted her face towards the sound, her eyes still closed. She felt the touch of Jamie's fingers as he brushed away the remnants of her tears. Then came the softer touch of his lips on her face. Gentle kisses that met each eye, each cheekbone, each corner of her mouth, before covering her lips.

Janet gasped at the painful intensity of awakened desire. As her lips parted she could taste the salt of her own tears on Jamie's lips and tongue. She could taste Jamie. She could drown in that taste. Her arms moved up around Jamie's neck automatically. He shifted his position, changing the angle of their contact so that no space was left between their bodies. Janet could feel his arousal matching her own. When his hand brushed slowly over her breast she cried out, the sound stifled by Jamie's questing mouth. He drew back slowly. They were both breathing hard, as though they'd run a considerable distance. Jamie had to clear his throat before he could speak, and his voice still sounded raw.

'Would the boys stay asleep…if we went upstairs?'

The boys. That was why Jamie was here. For a few minutes Janet had forgotten she was a mother. Had forgotten Jamie was a father. She had been aware of nothing but how much she wanted him. Was it her that Jamie wanted? Or was it simply gratitude that she'd capitulated over the issue of telling the boys the truth?

'I'm not sure,' she said untruthfully. The boys would sleep though anything short of the house collapsing around their ears. 'And I'm not sure this is a good idea, Jamie.' She pulled back and he released her reluctantly. Then he nodded slowly.

'You're right. It's certainly not why I came here.' Jamie's voice was well controlled now. 'We can do without any more complications. Let's deal with the most important issue. Do you want me to tell the boys myself or shall we do it together?'

Janet drew in a steadying breath. 'We'll do it together,' she said quietly. 'At the weekend. When we've all got plenty of time to talk things through.'

At least Janet could have a few more days to prepare herself. A few days to come to terms with the fact that she wasn't important in Jamie McFadden's life for her own sake. She was included solely because she was the mother of his children.

CHAPTER NINE

'JAMIE'S our dad? Our *real* dad?'

'That's right.' Janet was watching the boys carefully. She knew Jamie was staring at them just as intently from the other end of the kitchen table. They were just finishing a Saturday lunch of pizza and salad.

Adam and Rory looked at each other.

'Cool,' Adam stated calmly.

'Yeah,' Rory agreed. 'I told you he wasn't a dork.' He turned to Jamie. 'Are you going to live with us now?'

'No.' Jamie and Janet spoke in unison. Adam looked worried.

'Are you still going to take us to the Crusaders game?'

'You bet.' Jamie smiled. 'I'll be taking you lots of places.'

'What about when you go home?' Rory asked suspiciously. 'Mum said you might go back to Scotland one day.'

'Did she?' Jamie's quick glance at Janet was cool. 'Well, if I do, it will only be for a visit and you guys might even like to come with me.'

Janet stared at her plate. She'd like to go back to Scotland one day—just for a visit.

'For now, though,' Jamie continued, 'I'm going to

stay right here. I'm going to look for a house to buy and maybe you can come and stay the night sometimes.'

'Can Popeye and Olive come, too?'

'Sure.'

Adam caught his mother's eye. 'I'm full. Can we go and play now, Mum?'

'Aren't you going to eat your salad?'

'Salad sucks,' Rory announced.

'Rory!' Janet admonished.

'Salad's good for you,' Jamie said casually. 'It's my favourite.'

'Is it?' Rory turned an amazed gaze back to his plate. Adam folded up a lettuce leaf and chewed manfully. Rory still wasn't tempted. 'We're going to make a rat circus,' he said importantly. 'With a tightrope. Want to come and see, Jamie?' Rory stopped suddenly and angled his head speculatively. 'Hey! Do we get to call you "Dad" now?'

Jamie looked at each of his sons in turn. Janet's breathing tightened as she saw the glint of moisture in Jamie's eyes and heard the catch in his voice.

'I'd really like you to call me "Dad",' he told them. 'If you want to, that is.'

The boys raced out. Jamie and Janet sat in silence at their respective ends of the table. Their eye contact was sombre. The axis of all their lives had just tilted, despite the twins' apparently casual acceptance of the news. How was it going to affect them all in the long term? Janet felt the need to say something. Anything.

'You never used to like salad,' she commented.

'I still don't.' Jamie grinned. 'Salad sucks.'

The back door banged as the twins rushed back into the kitchen.

'Hey, Dad!' Rory yelled. 'Popeye and Olive have disappeared.'

'They chewed a big hole in the hutch,' Adam added forlornly. 'They've run away.'

Jamie stood up. 'I'll come and help you look for them,' he offered.

Janet watched them leave the room.

'Hey, Dad?' Rory said excitedly as they vanished from view. 'If we can't find them, can we have a dog instead?'

Everything had changed. And yet nothing had changed. The week at St David's settled into a normal routine. Sometimes chaotic, sometimes quiet. Some patients had serious problems to be dealt with but there were no major emergencies. Even the medical centre's more colourful patients were all behaving amenably.

Mr Collins demanded an appointment with Jamie. 'My blood feels a bit on the thin side,' he informed Sandy. 'I need to discuss my aspirin dose and I'm sure Dr McFadden's an expert on anticoagulation.'

Mrs Neville also had her sights set on the new doctor. She asked for a quiet word with Janet. 'I haven't talked to Dr Bennett yet about…you know, my little problem.'

'Haven't you?' Janet was surprised. 'Are the haemorrhoids getting better, then?'

'No.' Mrs Neville blushed. 'I've made an appointment with Dr McFadden this morning. He did such a good job with my finger and I thought…well…' Mrs Neville's colour deepened. 'I just wondered, could you have a word with him first? Before I go in?'

'Of course.' Janet patted the woman's arm. 'I'll make sure he understands and don't be embarrassed. Doctors are very used to dealing with problems like this.'

Constance Purdie came in for the regular dressing change on her ulcer. She wore a pair of startlingly pristine white trainers. Hope was wearing an identical pair of shoes.

'They're surprisingly comfortable,' she told Janet. 'I've joined a walking club.'

Constance poked Janet with a knobbly finger. 'There are lots of young men in that club,' she confided happily.

'Mother! You have to be over sixty-five to join.'

Janet told Jamie about Hope's potential younger man at morning tea. He chuckled. She then told him that she wasn't happy about administering May Little's psychiatric medications now that she'd been released from hospital. Jamie listened attentively.

'She's never been happy about needles,' Janet finished. 'Why does she have to have injectable drugs? She's going to be in here twice a week.'

'I'll do it.' Jamie grinned. 'As long as there are no cans of baked beans nearby.'

Pagan Ellis was bringing her baby in. The staff spent the rest of their break speculating enjoyably on what the little girl might have been called.

'Something astrological, I expect,' Oliver offered

finally. 'Probably Aquarius since she's so keen on water.'

'Dolphinia.' Sophie smiled. 'She likes dolphins as well.'

'What was the father's name?' Jamie queried.

'Ziggy,' Sophie supplied.

'Then it has to be Stardust.' Janet grinned. They were all laughing when Sandy came in to tell them that Pagan had arrived and could they all, please, come and admire the baby?

'What's the baby's name?' Sophie demanded.

Sandy looked at the expectant faces with surprise. 'Jane,' she told them. She looked even more puzzled at the wave of renewed mirth. 'What's so funny about that?'

'Never mind,' Jamie chuckled. 'It's a long story.' He caught Janet's eye and she smiled back. Funny how she'd once considered that Jamie didn't belong here. In a few short weeks he'd become as much part of the fabric of St David's as she was.

Jamie took an afternoon off on Wednesday to go house-hunting. A real estate agent had lined up several potential properties. He did the same thing the following week but didn't bother looking at more than the first house on offer that day.

'It's perfect,' he told Janet. 'Lovely big old house. Needs a bit of work but I've always fancied a project like that. It's got a swimming pool and half an acre of garden with a fantastic old pear tree that's just perfect for a tree hut.'

Janet had gone home trying to suppress waves of resentment. The house did sound perfect. Set up in a valley in the Cashmere Hills which was popular with market gardeners, it was only minutes away from town but still had a rural outlook. The house was big. The garden was huge. A swimming pool and a tree house to be installed. Jamie could offer the boys so much more than she could. How long would it be before they preferred the time they spent with their father?

Crusader fever hit town in a big way on Friday. Red and black balloons hung from shop windows, red and black streamers rippled from car aerials. A vehicle from a local radio station drove past St David's with 'Conquest of Paradise' blaring at deafening volume through the speakers attached to the roof. The staff speculated with considerable amusement what the effect might be when it drove past Mr Collins's residence. It wasn't the only excitement stirring the medical centre, however.

Oliver was grinning from ear to ear after a phone call. 'Josh and Toni are back in town. They want us all to meet for a drink tonight.' He slapped Jamie on the back. 'I've told them what a champion you are, mate, and they can't wait to meet you.' He turned to Janet. 'You'll come, won't you, Jan?'

'I'll have to see if I can get a babysitter,' Janet said. 'That's never been easy and I can't ask Mrs Carpenter any more.'

'I'll babysit for you,' Sandy offered. 'I'm too young to go to the pub.'

'Sold!' Oliver announced. 'See you there at seven, Janet.'

It was nearly 7.30, however, by the time Janet found a parking place and entered the bar the Coopers had chosen for the gathering. Toad Hall was known for its comfortable seating and casual atmosphere. Janet spotted Josh sitting on a couch with Jamie, engrossed in a conversation that was punctuated by frequent bursts of laughter. They had clearly taken an instant liking to each other. Janet found herself enveloped in an enthusiastic hug from Toni.

'It's so good to see you,' Toni said happily. 'I can't wait to get back to work. We've got some presents for Adam and Rory. We thought we'd save them until their birthday. It's not far away, is it?'

'Two weeks.' Janet nodded. Josh was standing up.

'My turn,' he announced, holding his arms open.

Janet laughed as she returned the warm embrace. 'You both look disgustingly brown and healthy.'

'I can recommend a good honeymoon,' Toni said with a smile. She turned to where Oliver and Sophie were sitting on another couch. 'It's poor Sophie who needs one now.' She squeezed onto the couch beside Sophie. 'I had a feeling you might be pregnant,' she said wistfully. 'Maybe it'll be my turn next.'

'We've been having a chat about Sophie,' Oliver told Janet. Josh had gone to the bar to get the glass of wine Janet had requested. 'We think she needs a good rest. At least a few weeks. Jamie's agreed to stay on.'

Janet nodded. 'That sounds sensible. Things should settle down by then.'

Oliver picked up his glass of beer. 'We're also toying with the idea of job sharing once this baby does arrive. Maybe there'll be a permanent position for Jamie one of these days.'

'If I get my registration,' Jamie said. 'What's that exam I have to sit?'

'The Primex,' Sophie reminded him. 'Don't worry, you'll breeze through. If I can do it, anyone can.' She reached for her glass of orange juice. 'We're having a double celebration here. I got my results through today.'

'You passed?' Janet's face lit up with pleasure. 'Congratulations, Sophie.'

'Thanks.' Sophie smiled at Jamie. 'You will, too. We'll have another celebration then.'

'I'll still need to apply for permanent residence,' Jamie said seriously. 'That might be more of a challenge.'

Janet accepted the glass of wine from Josh. He grinned at Jamie over his shoulder. 'You could always just marry a New Zealand citizen, mate. What's this we hear about you and Janet having a past history?'

There was a moment's awkward silence before Janet spoke.

'You're all going to find out one of these days so I may as well tell you now. Jamie is the twins' father.'

There was an even longer silence. Janet took a large gulp of her wine.

'Is that what brought you here, Jamie?' Toni asked finally. 'Did you want to see the boys again?'

'I didn't know the boys existed,' Jamie informed her flatly. 'Janet never even told me she was pregnant.'

Sophie was staring at Janet in dismay. 'You never said anything,' she accused. 'And there was Oliver and I thinking you wanted to keep them a secret because—' Sophie flushed scarlet as she realised the implication of her words. Jamie was now staring at her, frowning. He transferred the frown to Janet.

'I didn't want to keep them a secret.' Janet tried to sound offhand. 'I just wasn't ready to tell him straight away.'

'No. It took seven and a half years,' Jamie said lightly. 'I wonder how much longer it might have taken if I hadn't shown up.'

Janet could feel the shock waves coming from all directions. Sophie looked worried that she'd put her foot in it and hurt that Janet hadn't confided in her. Toni looked bemused, clearly wondering what sort of emotional minefield had been generated in her absence. Josh gave Jamie a sympathetic man-to-man type glance that conveyed the incomprehensibility of women. Oliver was frowning. Did he remember what Janet had told him about the father of the twins swanning off to get someone else pregnant?

'Are the boys your only children, Jamie?' he asked warily.

'They are indeed. I would have been bowled over to have found that I had one. Imagine how I felt to discover I had two.' He grinned and raised his glass. 'Here's to an instant family.'

'Twice as good,' Toni suggested.

'Two for the price of one.' Oliver chuckled.

'You could say that.' Jamie's glance caught Janet's. The atmosphere amongst the group had lost its heavy awkwardness but the look Janet received made her cringe inwardly. The price had been high. Jamie had support in his standpoint. Janet was the guilty party.

'So. Who's going to the rugby tomorrow?' Josh queried with an obvious move to change the subject. 'Thanks for getting us those tickets, Oliver. We'd better get home soon and shake off the jet lag so we don't fall asleep during the game.'

'Nobody falls asleep during a Crusaders match on home turf,' Oliver stated confidently. 'Are you going, Jamie?'

'Sure am.' Jamie's gaze clashed briefly with Janet's again. 'I'm taking my sons.'

The boys had never been so excited. They found it almost impossible to remain immobile long enough for Janet to apply their face-paint.

'If you want a black lightning bolt on red cheeks, you'd better stand still,' Janet warned Rory. She dipped a cotton bud into the pot of black paint and traced the outline of the zigzag carefully.

'Mine's going to be a red lightning bolt on black cheeks,' Adam told Jamie. He capered joyously around the kitchen.

'What's yours going to be, Dad?' Rory leapt out of the chair and Adam took his place. Janet used a sponge to put on the base layer of black paint.

'Oh, I don't think I need face-paint,' Jamie demurred. 'That's just for the kids, isn't it?'

'No.' Rory shook his head emphatically. '*Everybody* does it.'

'I'm wearing black jeans and a black sweatshirt and

I've got a red hat.' Jamie showed them his woollen cap. 'Isn't that enough?'

'No!' the twins shouted.

Adam admired his face in the hand mirror. 'Cool!'

'Paint Dad's face, Mum,' Rory commanded.

'OK. Sit there,' Janet directed. She picked up a sponge. 'What do you want to have?'

'Uh…' Jamie looked at the eager small faces watching him. 'I think I'll have one black cheek with red lightning and one red cheek with black lightning.'

The twins' faces lit up. Yet again Jamie was effortlessly performing like the hero he had become to the boys. Janet smoothed on the face-paint with the sponge. The red side had an uneven edge which she automatically stroked with her finger. She wished she hadn't. Touching Jamie's face kindled a spark of desire that not even the presence of two excited small children could diminish. Unnerved, Janet's gaze moved from Jamie's cheek to his eyes. The message was silent but crystal clear. He wanted her touch as much as she wanted to give it. But he could resist the urge. And he fully intended to resist it.

'Do the lightning bolts, Mum,' Rory directed. 'Hurry up.'

Adam was watching his mother. 'Why aren't you coming to the rugby, Mum?'

'I haven't got a ticket,' Janet said lightly. 'Come on. You'd better get going. The traffic will be awful.'

Janet stood outside to watch them climb into Jamie's car which had black and red balloons tied to the roof rack. Jamie hadn't even asked if she'd wanted a ticket, and Janet couldn't let the boys know how much the exclusion had hurt. She and the twins had been a complete family until Jamie had arrived. Now they were being split up on a regular basis. Janet knew she would have to get used to it. This was the way it was going to be from now on and the boys were too happy to give Janet reason to find fault with the arrangement.

They hadn't really been a complete family, anyway, had they?

Maybe they never would be.

CHAPTER TEN

'HAPPY birthday to us!'

'Happy birthday to us!'

The twins' voices carried up the stairs with bell-like clarity. Janet chuckled as she pulled her tight-fitting vest top over her head. She tucked the garment into the waistband of her denim shorts and then tightened the belt another two notches. She'd lost weight in the last month. Pining for something she couldn't have. Janet pulled a shirt from the wardrobe. A loose-fitting, soft cotton garment in her favourite dark delphinium blue. She left the shirt unbuttoned like a casual jacket and rolled the sleeves up to her elbows. It was going to be a hot day and the destination the boys had chosen for their birthday outing called for very casual comfort.

Adding the final touches to her make-up, Janet fluffed out her auburn curls and drew them back from her face with the blue headband that matched her shirt. She heard the decibel level increase downstairs.

'Dad! Dad! It's our *birthday*!'

The deep rumble of Jamie's voice didn't carry as well as the twins' piping tones. The burst of adult laughter made Janet pause long enough for another quick glance in her mirror. Did she look all right? Attractive even? Janet turned away with a sigh. It wouldn't make any difference. Jamie found her attractive enough physically. That had become increasingly obvious ever since the night she'd agreed to the twins learning the truth. But Jamie didn't want complications with the relationship he was forming with his children at last. And he still hadn't forgiven Janet for what he'd already missed.

Janet went downstairs slowly. The night after the rugby match had been the worst. The boys had been inspired by the robed horses which had led the Crusaders onto the rugby field. They'd been telling Jamie about the time they'd ridden a pony and wanted to show him the photographs of the occasion. They had all come out. All the baby photos, the mementos, the scrapbook of baby scribbles that Janet had proudly designated as artwork. Jamie had pored over them, asking endless questions even long after the twins had gone to bed. Then he'd become very quiet and Janet knew he'd been trying to absorb the impact of what he could never experience first hand. The withdrawal had been sustained for two weeks. Today was the first time Janet was to be included in the time Jamie spent with his sons.

Adam and Rory were standing in the kitchen, staring with round-eyed amazement as Jamie deposited yet another huge carton on the kitchen floor. The computer clearly had a lot of large components and Jamie had wrapped all the parcels to conceal the labelling.

'It's our birthday present,' Rory informed Janet in awed tones. 'Shall we open it now?'

Janet looked at the kitchen table. Her gifts to the boys still lay where the wrapping had been torn eagerly free. New school backpacks, red and black sweatshirts, ready for the next rugby match, and sets of felt pens. Small offerings compared with what their father was providing. Jamie was standing very still.

'What say we save it for when we get home?' he suggested. 'That way you can have fun guessing what might be inside the boxes.'

And the time lapse wouldn't allow for such a direct comparison of what each parent had offered. Janet gave Jamie a grateful smile.

'What a good idea. It's going to take a long time to open such big presents and if we don't get going we might miss having a swim while it's nice and hot.'

The boys had chosen to spend the day at Sumner Beach, a strip of coastline that bordered a popular seaside suburb of Christchurch. They planned to park at the Cave Rock end and then walk the length of the beach to the rock pools, playground and café. They would go home for a dinner of fish and chips and then discover what lay inside the mystery boxes. The guessing game as to the contents kept the boys amused for most of the car journey.

'The really big one could be a dog kennel,' Rory said hopefully, having exhausted the less appealing possibilities.

'And maybe there's a basket in another one,' Adam suggested, 'for an inside bed.'

'What about that smaller box?' Rory wondered. 'Do you think it might have a puppy in it?'

The twins regarded each other solemnly. They shook their heads sadly. 'It wasn't making any noise,' Adam pointed out.

Rory sighed. 'Maybe it's a very quiet puppy.'

'You're lucky your birthday is on a Saturday this year,' Jamie told the twins as they drove over the estuary bridge. 'Did you not want to bring any of your friends to your party?'

'No,' Adam said decisively. 'We wanted to go out with you *and* Mum. Like a proper family.'

Janet shut her eyes for a second. Anyone seeing the car go past would assume that was exactly what they were. Dad driving, Mum in the front passenger seat, two excited small children strapped firmly in the back.

'But we're not a *proper* family,' Rory informed his brother.

'Yes, we are,' Jamie asserted. 'We're very proper.'

'No,' Rory reiterated. 'We're not.'

'Why not?' Janet asked anxiously. She didn't want anything to spoil the day for her children. Adam tended to worry once Rory planted an undesirable theme.

'Because you and Dad aren't married.'

'Lots of parents aren't married,' Janet reminded him. 'Look at Michael. And Ben.'

'But they *were* married,' Rory stated. 'Ben's got the same name as *his* dad.'

'Why didn't you and Dad get married, Mum?' Adam sounded worried already.

Janet turned so she could look at the boys. 'It just didn't happen that way,' she said carefully. 'Your dad had another job to go to a long way away.'

'I wasn't given the opportunity.' Jamie broke his protracted silence as he turned the car onto the espla-

nade and eased into a parking slot. Janet frowned. Did
he want the boys to join the numbers that considered
her to be at fault?

'Dad had another girlfriend,' she said lightly. 'He
liked her more.'

'Did you?' Rory demanded. Both boys stared at
Jamie with disbelief.

'No, of course not.' Jamie flicked Janet an angry
glance. 'Your mum just thought I did.'

'Why did you think that, Mum?' Adam sounded
puzzled.

'Because the other girl told me,' Janet said. It
sounded like a weak excuse now, even to her.

'Did you *believe* her?' Rory asked. 'How did you
know she wasn't telling a lie?'

'I did believe her, I'm afraid,' Janet said sadly.
'Then.' She looked at Jamie. Would he understand
that she was trying to reach out? To apologise?

Jamie was looking straight ahead. 'Look at that
rock!' he exclaimed. 'It's bigger than my new house.
Is that where the cave is?'

Adam and Rory were instantly distracted. 'If the
tide's out you can go right through and there's rock
pools and everything. And you can climb up the outside to the top. Can we climb up, Mum? Please?'

'It's very high.' Janet peered at the unforgiving,
steep slopes of the rock formation. 'I think you're still
a bit young for that.'

'*Please*, Mum! You've never let us and it's our
birthday. Dad can come with us. He'll look after us.'

Jamie finally made eye contact with Janet. 'That's
right,' he said seriously. 'I'll look after them.'

Janet collected the backpacks from the car and checked their contents—buckets and spades, spare shorts and towels, cold drinks, bags of crisps and fruit. She sat on the white sand and watched the small crowd swarming over the rock. It was easy to pick out Jamie and the twins. The identical golden heads bobbed energetically and shone in the bright sunlight. Janet fished in one of the bags to find their sun hats. By the time she'd unearthed the bottle of sunscreen they were all on their way down from the summit. She could see the protective way Jamie was guiding and assisting the children. They reached the sand without so much as a graze and hauled Janet to her feet.

'Come on, Mum! We're going to see the cave and then we want a swim.'

The boys found a starfish in a rock pool. It was Jamie they rushed to first to show off the treasure. They spotted two black Labradors frolicking in the surf. It was Jamie's hands they tugged.

'Look, Dad! Twins—just like us!'

'Can we get a dog, Mum? *Please?*'

Janet looked helplessly at Jamie. He grinned. 'Maybe.'

The boys stripped down to their shorts for a swim. So did Jamie. They all eyed Janet.

'Aren't you coming for a swim?' Jamie queried.

'I didn't bring my togs,' Janet said regretfully. She had decided against it, aware of how exposed she would feel in Jamie's company. Now she felt excluded and, instead of the distraction of playing in the surf, she would have to sit and watch the sleek, near nakedness of the man she desperately wanted. The boys were already running towards the water. 'Don't go out too far,' Janet shouted.

The sun had climbed to its zenith by the time they began the long walk along the firm stretch of sand the ebb tide had uncovered. The boys alternately dashed in and out of the shallows and dawdled beside the adults. Adam finally remembered that he had something to worry about.

'Why weren't we born in Scotland?' he wanted to know.

'Because I came to live here while you were still in my tummy,' Janet answered with an inward sigh. She could sense Jamie's tension as his long stride lost its relaxed swing.

'Why?' Adam demanded.

'Yeah, why?' Rory echoed. 'I wish we were Scottish—like Dad.'

'I came because I felt sad,' Janet said quietly. She had always tried to answer her children's questions honestly. They knew when they were being fobbed off. A seagull swooped overhead, its mournful cry adding appropriate depth to Janet's admission.

'Why did you feel sad?' Adam asked in surprise. 'Didn't you know you were having us?'

'Yes, I did know.' Janet reached out and ruffled Adam's curls. 'That made me happy. I was sad because it's not very nice when you love someone and they don't love you back.'

'You mean Dad?' Rory asked. His head swung towards Jamie. 'Didn't you love Mum, Dad?'

Jamie cleared his throat. 'I loved her very much,'

he told Rory. 'I think I loved her more than she loved me.'

'How do you know that?' Adam nearly stumbled as he tried to peer earnestly up into Jamie's face.

'Because I believed her but she didn't believe me.'

'Why didn't you believe Dad, Mum?'

Janet smiled wistfully and shook her head. She had no good answer to that question. Not any more.

'Did you know we were going to be born, Dad?'

'No.' Jamie sounded as sad as Janet felt. 'Your mum never told me.'

'I *tried* to,' Janet said softly. 'I got told something that changed my mind.'

'What?'

'Just things,' Janet said evasively. Honesty with children could only go so far. 'Do you want to look in the rock pools or have lunch first?'

'Rock pools!' the twins shouted. They raced off, leaving Jamie and Janet walking alone.

'What things,' Jamie asked quietly, 'did you get told?'

'I rang you...in London,' Janet said reluctantly. 'Sharlene answered the phone. She told me she was living there. She said she was pregnant and was sure she could trap the father into marrying her.'

'She did,' Jamie confirmed. 'Poor Paul had been very careful not to let her know where he was living, but when she turned up he couldn't ignore the fact that she was pregnant. They got divorced about a year later.'

'Who?' Janet frowned in confusion.

'Sharlene and Paul—the surgeon I was flatting

with.' Jamie stopped and gripped Janet's arm. 'Did she say it was *my* baby?'

Janet shook her head. 'I guess she didn't use any names. I just assumed...'

Jamie shook his head in disgust. 'It all goes back to the same thing. You didn't trust me.'

'Sharlene *told* me she was sleeping with you,' Janet said angrily. 'She had to be telling the truth. She knew about that birthmark beside your—'

'For God's sake, Janet,' Jamie broke in. 'Did you not have any idea what sort of reputation Sharlene had? She was a prize nuisance around Theatre. Always hanging around when we were getting changed. Eyeing us over like slabs of prime beef. Of course she would have known about the birthmark. She practically used a magnifying glass.'

Janet laughed but she was perilously close to tears. 'I had no idea. I just knew she was determined to marry a doctor.' Janet searched Jamie's face. 'But you knew about the letter she wrote me.'

'What letter?'

'Telling me she was going to get married. That she wanted her things sent down because she'd need to shift before the baby arrived.'

'I didn't know anything about her writing to you,' Jamie claimed. 'I was talking about *my* letter. The one I sat up writing all night the day before I left for London.'

'What letter?' Janet whispered. 'I never got one.'

'Of course you did,' Jamie said angrily. 'I gave it to Sharlene and she promised to give it to you.' His face changed as he stared at Janet.

'I never got it,' Janet reiterated. 'Why would she have done something like that?'

Jamie shrugged. 'Maybe she was keeping me for back-up in case things didn't work out with Paul. Maybe she read it first and was too embarrassed to hand it over. Who knows? Who cares?'

'I do.' Janet shaded her eyes as she looked for the twins. They were bent over a rock pool within easy shouting distance. Janet turned back to Jamie. 'What did you say? In the letter?'

Jamie was also watching the twins. He waved as they looked up. The boys waved back briefly, before returning their attention to the pool. Rory was pointing excitedly at something. Adam crouched, extending his arm into the water. Jamie kept his gaze on the children as he spoke wearily.

'I said I loved you. That I didn't want to live without you. That I wanted the chance to prove your trust hadn't been misplaced. I said that I was sorry if I'd given you any impression that your possible pregnancy was a serious obstacle to our future together.' Jamie took a deep breath. 'I said I wanted to marry you and I gave you the address and phone number at my flat in London.'

Jamie caught Janet's eye. She gave a small gasp. 'That was how Sharlene knew where you were. Where Paul had gone!'

Jamie shrugged. 'I guess.' He held the eye contact. 'I ended the letter by saying I'd leave it up to you. If I didn't hear anything I'd know there was no future for us.'

'Oh.' Janet could think of nothing more to say. No

wonder Jamie thought it had been her fault. It *had* been her fault.

'I resisted trying to find you for a couple of weeks,' Jamie continued bitterly. 'But I couldn't keep it up. I rang and rang that damned nurses' home. I finally got an answer and somebody said they'd pass on a message—if they saw you. Then Sharlene turned up at the flat. She told me you'd gone to New Zealand. She had no idea of a forwarding address. I was angry that you could have given up on me so easily. I gave up at that point.'

The twins were racing towards them. They held their hands outstretched.

'*Crabs!*' they shrieked. '*Look!*'

Janet and Jamie looked and admired the tiny specimens. The boys put them in a bucket with some seawater, ignoring the adults' warnings that the crabs wouldn't survive if they took them home. They let the boys show them the anemones in the rock pool, find some more crabs and attempt to prise limpets off the rocks before hunger sent them all up to the outdoor café for a lunch of hot chips and ice creams.

Janet found herself catching Jamie's glance at frequent intervals. She was still trying to absorb what they had both learned, wondering whether it could make a difference to Jamie's judgement of her. It still didn't alter the fact that he'd been denied his sons' early years. But was it enough to allow him to forgive her?

The playground held the twins' interest for nearly an hour after the late lunch. Then they began to meander slowly back along the beach towards Cave Rock and the car.

'Have you had a good time?' Janet asked the twins.

'Yeah.' Rory transferred the bucket of crabs to his left hand, using his right hand to catch hold of one of Jamie's hands. Adam claimed the other one, before taking hold of Janet's hand as well. The four walked together, hands linked, their arms swinging in a gently co-ordinated rhythm.

'Are you happy you have us?' Rory asked Jamie suddenly.

'I couldn't be happier,' Jamie said seriously.

'Were you surprised to find there were two of us?'

'It was twice as good,' Jamie assured Adam.

Rory grinned cheerfully. 'Mum says we're twice as much trouble.'

'That's true.' Janet laughed. 'But it doesn't change how much I love you.'

'Even when we're *really* naughty?'

'Even then,' Janet confirmed. 'You can be very cross with people if they do silly things, but if you really love them you can forgive them anything. You never stop loving them.' Her eyes met Jamie's across the top of Adam's head.

'Do *you* love us, Dad?' Rory asked earnestly.

'Sure do.' Jamie nodded.

'But you loved Mum, too, didn't you?'

'Yes, I did.'

'And you really loved Dad, didn't you, Mum?'

'Yes,' Janet affirmed quietly. 'I did.'

'Mum did something naughty, didn't she, Dad?'

Adam was carefully following his line of logic. 'Not telling you about us.'

Janet swallowed painfully. Out of the mouths of children, she thought. The blame still rested with her.

'I did something naughty, too,' Jamie told the boys. 'It wasn't just Mum's fault.'

'But did that stop you loving each other?'

Janet and Jamie's eyes met again. They spoke together. 'No.'

Adam nodded, finally satisfied. Rory wasn't.

'So why can't we be a proper family, then, and have a dog?'

Jamie smiled slowly at Janet. She drank in the message she was receiving and smiled back. She could feel tears of pure happiness gathering, misting her vision. There *was* hope. More than hope.

'We'll talk about it,' Jamie promised. 'Why don't you go and let those poor crabs go in those rocks up there? When the tide comes in they'll be able to go home.'

The boys wandered off, too tired to run any more. Jamie's eyes were fastened on Janet's face.

'It's true,' he said softly. 'I never stopped loving you.'

'I never stopped loving you,' Janet echoed.

Jamie caught both Janet's hands. 'Do you think the twins are right? That we could be a proper family and have a dog?'

Janet smiled shakily. 'Being parents is good.'

Jamie grinned. 'Being married might be twice as good.' He pulled Janet into his arms. 'Shall we find out, Janna? Try being a proper family?'

Janet didn't need to answer. She couldn't answer as Jamie's lips claimed hers. She wound her arms around his neck, knowing her body could answer him far more effectively than any words. They were together at last. All of them.

'Look at that!' Rory looked up from the rock pool and poked his brother excitedly. 'Mum and Dad are being *really* naughty!'

Adam caught Rory's eye and grinned. The twins both spoke together.

'*Cool!*'

The World of
Mills & Boon®

There's a Mills & Boon® series that's perfect
for you. We publish ten series and, with new
titles every month, you never have to wait
long for your favourite to come along.

Blaze.

Scorching hot, sexy reads
4 new stories every month

By Request

*Relive the romance with
the best of the best*
9 new stories every month

Cherish™

*Romance to melt the
heart every time*
12 new stories every month

Desire™

*Passionate and dramatic
love stories*
8 new stories every month